A TEMPLAR BOOK

First published in the UK in 2014 by Templar Publishing,
an imprint of The Templar Company Limited,
Deepdene Lodge, Deepdene Avenue,
Dorking, Surrey, RH5 4AT, UK

www.templarco.co.uk

ISBN 978-1-84877-927-3

eISBN 978-1-78370-021-9

Printed in the UK

NO GOING BACK

ALEX GUTTERIDGE

templar

For Vika, with love.

When you love someone,
you love the whole person,
just as he or she is,
and not as you would
like them to be.

Leo Tolstoy

THE END

In a second your life can change. One careless moment and everything that you have ever known and trusted has gone.

I was four years old and sitting at the top of the stairs, hidden just around the dog-leg, my knees pressed up tightly against my chest. It was a hot, airless August night and I was wearing my favourite pink brushed-cotton nightie. It had embroidered rosebuds on the collar, which buttoned right up under my chin, and the material was way too hot for the time of year. Perhaps that's why I couldn't sleep, or perhaps I sensed that something was wrong. I can't exactly remember. It's too long ago.

I remember that Dad had promised to read me a bedtime story and he'd never broken his promises before. We were halfway through *Winnie the Pooh* and I couldn't wait to hear about Pooh building

 9

a house for Eeyore. When Dad was late, Mum put me to bed, but I didn't stay there for long. I could hear her in the hall, pacing, then ringing around, trying to track him down. There was a knot in my stomach which, with each futile phone call, got tighter and tighter and bigger and bigger. I wanted to leave the stairs and go down and sit on Mum's knee, to wrap my arms around her neck, to feel her reassuring kisses. But I didn't dare. She was strict with bedtimes, so instead I crept back up to my bedroom to fetch my favourite teddy, the one Dad had brought back from a business trip to Ireland when I was a baby. In those days Teddy always made everything better.

When the doorbell rang I slid down the top three steps to get a better look through the gaps under the dark oak banisters. The plum-coloured carpet scraped against my bottom. Mum flung open the front door and immediately her hands flew up to her face like a couple of fluttering, startled birds.

"No!"

Such a small word but she gasped it out, as if the effort of saying it had taken all of her breath.

The policeman teetered on the threshold, the tips

of his shiny shoes inside the house, heels still embedded in the golden gravel path.

"Mrs Cooper? Can we come in?"

The questions were innocent enough but I knew from the gravity of his tone and the stiffness of his fingers as they splayed against the side of his leg that he was about to say something I didn't want to hear. I put my hands over my ears and pressed my face down between my knees. The nightdress was soft against my cheeks, like a well-worn comfort blanket, and it smelled of vanilla fabric softener. In my mind I tried to make the policeman go away but when I lifted my head and opened my eyes he was still there, guiding Mum back into our house as if she were the stranger. Even before the WPC followed him in and insisted that Mum sat down on the sofa, even before the policeman said, "I'm afraid there's been an accident," I knew that my daddy wasn't ever coming back.

ROOTS

After the funeral Gran wanted Mum to move back to Derbyshire.

"What on earth do you want to stay in London for?" she asked. "It isn't the right place to bring up a child on your own."

Mum gathered me close, made me feel almost safe again. Just for a moment.

"It's Laura's home," she'd said, over the top of my head. "I'm not uprooting her, not now. This is where her memories are."

Of course, that wasn't the end of it. Gran doesn't like taking no for an answer. Every now and then she'd bring it up, try to make Mum feel as if she was being a bad mother by not taking me back to 'where we belonged'. But my mum doesn't like being told what to do either and for ten whole years she stood her ground. She did waver when Grandad died though. I was twelve by then and more than old enough to know that it was wrong to wish that Gran had gone first.

"Perhaps we ought to move back, Laura," Mum had said, as we drove home down the M1 after a strange weekend at the farm when I kept expecting Grandad to walk through the door in his brown overalls and envelop me in one of his big, strong, earthy-smelling hugs. "Gran's not getting any younger."

I studied the spray from the lorry in front and gripped the sides of the seat. Since Dad's accident motorways always made me edgy. "She's got Aunt Jane," I replied. "She's only at the other end of the village and we're not that far away. We visit loads as well."

Mum indicated and pulled into the middle lane to overtake. My tongue fixed itself to the roof of my mouth.

"It's not the same though," she said. "If something happened and we were closer…"

"Grandad had a massive heart attack," I interrupted. Forcing myself to say those words

13

made my own heart miss a beat. Losing Grandad so suddenly had felt like being dropped out of a plane into some frozen wilderness. For days I felt as if I were in this bizarre bubble. I was totally alone in a strange, unfriendly place with no one to guide me. I should have known how to cope because I'd been through something similar before. But that didn't make it any better. If anything it probably made it worse. Mum was in pieces too and I tried to comfort her. It was Grandad who understood us both the best. He was the one who showed us and told us how much he loved us every single time we saw or spoke to him and I realised, once he'd gone, that maybe we hadn't said those same words back. Not often enough anyway. I swallowed, put my hand to my chest where there seemed to be this void.

"If we'd been living next door to the farm it wouldn't have been near enough to make a difference," I said softly.

I sensed Mum wince.

"No, you're right," she said, reaching for a bottle of water.

"Mum! Please keep both hands on the wheel."

14

Momentarily, she turned her head and looked at me. "Sorry." She bypassed the water bottle and rested the tips of her fingers on my black leggings.

"Mum!" I screeched, lifting her hand and slapping it back where it belonged. "Besides," I continued, making a deliberate effort to lower my tone, to sound less of a nutcase. "I like where we live, and it suits us, doesn't it? You've got your job. I've got my friends…" I paused, felt that familiar tightness in my chest, "… and then there's Dad."

She didn't reply but, in the half-light, I saw her French-manicured nails wrap right around the steering wheel until they dug into her palms.

"Who would put flowers on his grave every week?" I said. "If we moved away it would feel as if we were leaving Dad behind." My voice dropped to a whisper. "I couldn't do that, not ever. You wouldn't want to do that either, would you, Mum? Not really?"

She sighed, gave me a brief sideways glance.

"One day, Laura, you might have to move away, for your job or if you get married. One day you're going to have to—"

"Don't say 'move on'," I snapped, "or I'll think Gran has hypnotised you. She won't forget Grandad, will she, so why does she want me to forget all about my dad?"

"Laura, that's very unkind and not fair," Mum shot out. "No one's suggesting that you forget your father."

"Really?"

My sarcasm sliced through the air as efficiently as the wiper blade despatched the rain from the windscreen.

"Are you telling me that Gran doesn't want *you* to 'move on', Mum, to find someone else? That's all she seems to talk about since Dad died – that and us moving out of London."

Mum brushed a strand of hair away from her face. "Gran just wants us both to be happy," she said softly. "That's all."

"Yeah right," I murmured. "But Gran's happiness manual seems to include the rule 'pretend that Dad didn't exist'."

The car swerved slightly as someone came past us very fast and I heard Mum suck in her breath.

I sank down in my seat and made a deliberate show of putting in my earphones. This was one of those conversations that wasn't going anywhere and the last thing my nerves needed was a good old row to take Mum's mind off the road. One fatal crash in the family was more than enough to cope with.

CHANGE

Things settled down for a while. I suppose 'the calm before the storm' is how Grandad would have described it. It was two years later when things really changed. I had just turned fourteen. Grandad always used to say that things happen in threes. So when the boiler packed up on the coldest day of winter I suspected that there was worse to come. Too true. Two weeks later Mum lost her job and three days after that Gran fell off the ladder.

The phone rang at teatime. It was a Wednesday and I'd just served up my signature dish – pasta with an aubergine and tomato sauce. There's a really cool greengrocers near our school with all of the produce artfully arranged in wicker baskets and inside they even have a blackboard with recipes chalked up. As soon as I was allowed to walk to and from school on my own, Mum often asked me to pick things up for supper. So that day I'd stopped off and bought two glossy purple aubergines, some red onions and a garlic. Back at home, I chopped up the vegetables and roasted them in olive oil so that they were ready for when Mum got back from her appointment at the job centre. All we had to do was add some sundried tomatoes and a few basil leaves, and heat it through while the linguine was cooking. This was one of Mum's favourite meals and I'd wanted to surprise her, to try to wipe that worried look off her face. Mum's an underwear designer and she wasn't hopeful about finding another job that paid as well as the last one, so I knew that aubergines and mega-expensive sundried tomatoes might have to be scratched off the shopping list in the future.

"This is lovely, Laura," Mum said, taking her first mouthful. "Thank you. It's just what I needed."

The ring of the phone interrupted my smile.

Mum groaned. Her fork, loaded with pasta, hovered in front of her lips.

"It'll just be someone trying to sell you something," I said.

She nodded and carried on eating but perhaps

the ring sounded more urgent than usual. As she twirled her second forkful of linguine, she sighed, put down her fork and reached out.

"Hi, Jane, is everything all right?"

I stopped chewing and glanced at the clock: 5.45 p.m. Aunt Jane never rang at this time. She should be cooking supper, sorting out homework, stopping the boys from fighting, trying to get Liberty to help her tidy up. Fat chance there, I thought with a wry smile.

It's amazing how different two cousins could be and still be best friends. Liberty's three months older than me but I'm the neat freak, a 'place for everything, everything in its place' sort of girl, whereas Liberty's far more diva than domesticated. She's an expert at lying on the sofa watching her favourite reality TV show or reading a magazine while jobs demand to be done and chaos reigns around her.

She's also the next best thing I've got to a sister. My dad didn't want any more children. Mum said that he didn't think it would be fair to have another baby as he couldn't possibly love another child as much as he loved me. When she told me that I felt really special but deep down I'd still have liked a sibling. At least I had Liberty. Even though we lived one hundred and fifty miles apart we Facebooked and texted each other all the time. So despite the fact that we didn't see each other every day, or even every week, I felt really close to her. I also felt lucky because we seemed to be closer than some sisters. I never thought that we'd ever fall out with one another, not big time.

"When...? Where...? What on earth...?"

Only the beginnings of questions left Mum's lips. At the other end of the line I could hear the quick, high-pitched, panic-stricken tone of Aunt Jane's voice. Bad news was spilling out of the phone into our kitchen and the pasta began to set like cardboard ribbons in our bowls. Mum pushed back her fringe, never a good sign, and looked at her watch.

"I'll come – we can be there by ten."

Dismay gave the sauce a bitter taste in my mouth. I pushed my bowl away. On Friday there was a school trip to the fashion exhibition at the V&A. I'd been looking forward to it for ages. If we went up to Derbyshire that night I knew we'd end up staying for the weekend.

"Well, if you're absolutely sure?"

Mum's doubtful tone dragged me back from the glamour of French couture and I tore a basil leaf into shreds, willing Aunt Jane to pile on more of the older sister pressure and tell her not to worry, that she was in control of whatever crisis was taking place. Mum walked to the window and looked out into the darkness. I felt really selfish for thinking of myself first but sometimes you just can't help yourself, can you?

"Okay," Mum said, after what seemed like a pause worthy of the *Guinness Book of World Records*. "We'll see you on Friday evening then. But if there's any change, you will tell me straight away?"

Mum's hand shook as she placed the phone back in its cradle. "Oh my goodness. I knew this would happen sooner or later."

She sank back onto the chair, all colour drained from her face. She looked as if she'd seen a ghost.

"Gran's had an accident."

I tried to look as concerned as I should have felt but guilt prevented me from making eye contact.

"Is she all right?"

Mum's eyes were bright with tears. Her fringe stood out from her forehead like one of those ancient, frayed sweeping brushes that Uncle Pete uses on the farm.

"Yes and no. She's broken her hip and is in hospital in Derby. They're hoping to operate tomorrow."

I tore off a piece of cold garlic bread and lifted it to my lips. I was still hungry. That wasn't normal, was it? Surely the shock, the upset, should have robbed me of my appetite?

"How did that happen?"

Mum closed her eyes, as if imagining the moment.

"She was up a ladder, decorating."

Her lids flipped open and she stared straight at me.

"How many times have I told her not to do that, to get someone in? It's not as if she can't afford it."

I chewed, shrugged, leaned forwards, touched Mum's arm. Tears spilled down her face.

I leaned over and pulled a tissue from the box

on the work surface, handed it to her.

"You know Gran, she's never been one to take advice. I'm sure she'll be okay."

Mum dabbed at her cheek, making little holes in her foundation.

"Your Auntie Jane says there's no point going at the moment. We might as well wait until the weekend."

She managed a weak smile.

"At least you won't have to miss your trip to the V&A."

The garlic bread stuck in my throat. I thought she'd forgotten.

"Why don't you go up anyway?" I offered. "I could always spend a couple of nights with Chloe and get the train on Saturday."

She shook her head. "No, Friday will be fine. We can go straight to the hospital and then we can spend a couple of days deciding what's going to happen next."

I coughed, drank some water.

"Next?" I croaked.

A crumb of bread stuck persistently to the side of my throat.

"Well, someone's going to have to look after Gran when she comes out of hospital. She won't be able to manage on her own for a while," Mum said.

So that was the start of it. We went up to Derbyshire on that Friday night and I wonder if Mum had already decided our future then – or maybe it was the row with Aunt Jane that settled it. That and the fact that Gran didn't recover nearly as well as everyone expected.

THE BOMBSHELL

It was the May bank holiday when Mum dropped the bombshell. We were back in Derbyshire *again*. We'd barely had a weekend at home since Gran's accident. Anyway there we were in Aunt Jane's bewilderingly messy kitchen. How anyone can live with all of that stuff taking over the work surfaces I can't imagine. I want to clear it all away, find homes for all of the pots and pans, the straggle of herb and spice jars, the unemptied supermarket bags. The weird thing is that they don't even seem to notice how untidy it is.

That day the boys had been banished to the garden, as if they were the ones cluttering up the space. Liam and Luke are only eighteen months apart in age. Aunt Jane had several miscarriages after Liberty was born and everyone thought she wouldn't be able to have any more children. Then, six years later, along came

Liam, closely followed by Luke. I reckon I was just as excited as Liberty to have babies in the family. They seem to love me like a sister too. Sometimes though they won't leave me alone, so on that particular day it was a bit of a relief that they'd been sent outside to let off steam because it meant that Liberty and I could sit quietly on the sofa playing cards.

"We can't go on like this," Uncle Pete said. "Jane's been working herself into the ground since your mother came out of hospital. This is the second migraine she's had in a week."

Mum moved towards the kettle. "I'll take her up some tea."

"Your sister doesn't need tea," Uncle Pete shouted. "She needs help."

I looked across at Liberty. She kept her eyes firmly fixed on the cards.

"I'm doing what I can," Mum replied softly.

"Well I'm sorry, Liz, but it's not enough."

My hand hovered in mid-air. I was holding the ten of diamonds. Those diamonds seemed to blur into a mass of red in front of my eyes. The kitchen was suddenly uncharacteristically still. It felt as if the whole house was waiting for something. Outside there was the sound of a football being kicked. *Thud, thud, thud* like a slowed-down heartbeat. Uncle Pete's eyes were bulging, his body squared up as if ready for a fight.

"If you won't do more, we'll have to get someone in – or Margaret will have to go into a home and you have *no* idea how much that will cost."

"Oh yes I do," Mum flashed back. "But that's not what I want and I don't think it's necessary."

"I'm just looking for practical solutions to the problem," Uncle Pete replied.

Mum's chin was lifted, her jaw set. "She's *my* mother. She's not a problem and *that* is not the answer."

"Well, what is?" Heads swivelled to where Aunt Jane stood in the doorway, wearing a fluffy pink dressing gown, dark circles under her eyes. She walked to the table and sank onto a chair, Uncle Pete immediately resting his hands on her shoulders.

"It's all right for you swanning up here at the weekend," she said to Mum. "Mother's so pleased to see you that she makes a special effort. You don't get all of the moaning, the depression. You don't bear the brunt of it. And after a couple of days you just go back to your normal life without a care in the world."

For a few seconds I was shell-shocked. Where had all this come from? I knew that the tension had been building since Gran's accident but I wasn't prepared for this. Obviously neither was Mum.

"You know that's not true," she said quietly.

For about the millionth time in my life I wished that Dad was here. He wouldn't have let them talk to Mum like that. But he wasn't, so, without looking at Liberty, I placed my cards down on the green linen cushion and went to stand next to Mum. She leaned against me slightly.

"I may not have a job at the moment but I've got Laura to think of," she said. "I can't just pull her out of school in the middle of term."

"That's right," Aunt Jane retorted, "use Laura as a way of avoiding your responsibilities. Let's face it, that's why you've stayed in London all these years, so you don't have to deal with any of the difficult stuff."

I felt Mum flinch. "That's not fair." The words spurted out of me with the suddenness of one of those Icelandic geysers we'd studied in geography. Everyone stared at me in surprise, everyone except Liberty. She had studiously begun to play clock patience on the coffee table in front of her.

"Stay out of this, Laura," Uncle Pete warned. "It's nothing to do with you."

"It's got everything to do with me," I shouted. "We've been coming up here every weekend for weeks to help out and do you appreciate it? No!" I glared at my aunt and uncle. "It's not all about you, you know."

Uncle Pete was purple in the face now and Aunt Jane had twisted to grab hold of his arm.

"That's enough, Laura," Mum murmured. She moved to the table and sat down, opposite Aunt Jane.

"You *are* right about one thing," she said, sounding calmer than she looked. "We can't go on like this, so I think the best thing is if we move up here at the beginning of the summer holidays. Can you manage until then?"

Even then I didn't realise what she was saying. No one did.

"I suppose we'll have to," Aunt Jane replied ungraciously.

"And what if six weeks isn't enough?" Uncle Pete added. "What if your mother still isn't back on her feet? What if she never gets back to how she was before?"

Mum traced her finger over a knot in the pine table. She looked up, but at them, not at me.

She should have looked at me, given me some warning. We were a team, that's what she used to say and I believed her. I trusted her completely. If you're part of a team you consult each other, don't you? You don't have any secrets, or that's what I thought. I was in complete ignorance as I stood behind her chair. There wasn't a voice in my head that said, *Brace yourself, Laura. Things are about to change. Big time.* That's what made everything so much worse: the fact that I wasn't prepared.

"I wasn't talking about just moving up here for the holidays," Mum said. "I meant for good."

My mouth dropped open. I could hardly believe it. But instantly I knew it was true. Once Mum made up her mind about something that was it. The wheels had been set in motion. There was no going back.

FLOWERS

We didn't speak all the way back to London. As we pulled up outside our house, the light from the hall shone through the stained glass window at the top of the front door. Mum always had the lamp on an automatic timer and I loved the welcoming glow it gave when we arrived home after dark. The glass picture was of a beautiful blue boat balanced on little curly waves and, at that moment, I just wanted to sail away to a desert island, away from everyone and everything.

"Laura, come on! It's late and you've got school tomorrow."

Mum opened the passenger door and held my overnight bag out to me. I grabbed it, slammed the car door shut and followed her up the garden path, keeping my head down. As soon as the front door was open I pushed past her, pulled off my trainers and left them where they landed in an easy-to-trip-over place.

"I'll get something to eat," Mum said, dropping her keys with a familiar clink into the little turquoise bowl on the radiator shelf.

"Yeah right," I replied, climbing the stairs. "Food, that'll solve everything, won't it?"

I heard her suck in her breath, sensed her using a heroic amount of willpower to prevent the snap back.

"Just some toast and a hot drink?" she called after me. Persuasively. Verging on pleading.

"Don't bother," I shouted, slamming my bedroom door even harder than the car door, so hard that my best photo of Dad collapsed face down on the bedside table. I flung myself face down on the bed in sympathy, pulling the pillow over my head. Two minutes later I heard a muffled *tap, tap, tap*.

"Laura, can I come in?"

Too late to say no. She was already there, tilting the mattress as she perched on the edge of my bed, her hand resting lightly on my shoulder.

"I'm sorry, Laura. I didn't mean for it to come out like that."

I didn't reply. She waited. Grown-ups are good at that. Waiting. It was getting hot under that pillow and I couldn't breathe properly. I had to emerge eventually, didn't I?

"So how did you mean for it to come out then, Mum?" I mumbled, turning onto my side, half lifting the pillow, feeling the dampness where sweat had stuck my hair to the nape of my neck. "When were you going to tell me about all of these plans you've been making behind my back?"

"It's not like that, Laura. I'm just trying to do what's best for everyone."

I turned around properly then, propped myself up on my elbows, felt the anger, boiling hot, inside of me.

"Not for me you're not. Were you even going to ask what *I* wanted?"

She shifted, bent down, picked a piece of fluff up from the carpet.

"It's not a decision that I've made on a whim. I've been thinking about it for a while, even before I lost

34

my job, even before Gran broke her hip. I'll be forty in a couple of years, Laura, and you're growing up fast. You'll have your own life, away from here. If we're going to make a change, now is as good a time as any."

"And what about school, my friends, the house? What about Dad? We're the only family he had. Who will look after the grave if we're not here?"

"You can move school and Derbyshire's not that far. You can come back and see your friends. We'll come back and keep an eye on the grave too."

"Every week or two?"

"No, but—"

"He wouldn't have wanted you to do this to me. He wouldn't have wanted you to take me away from where I grew up, from everything I know. This is my home, Mum. It's our home."

My throat felt all tight and my voice was horribly high-pitched.

"Oh, Laura." Mum stood up, sadness sweeping across her face. "You have no idea what your father would have wanted. You think you do, but..." She shrugged, stood up and moved towards the

35

door. "I'm not going to change my mind about this. The move will be good for us, you wait and see." I flung myself over to face the wall and clamped my hands over my ears. I didn't want to hear any more. I just wanted to pretend it wasn't happening.

We weren't selling the house, just renting it out. That was something, I suppose. Some small bit of hope to grasp hold of. It meant that one day we might be able to come back. In the meantime someone else would be sleeping in my bed, sitting at our kitchen table, sunning themselves on our little bit of decking. I hated that and I hated them, whoever they were, and I hated Mum. At least I pretended I did. Those last few weeks in London were horrible. I wanted to enjoy myself, to make the most of everything, but whatever I did felt spoiled. Part of me wanted to be in the house all the time (but not when Mum was there), but the other part of me couldn't bear to mooch around listening to the imaginary clock in my head ticking down to the day we'd close the gate for the last time. So I went out – a lot. If my friends weren't around I visited Dad's grave. Sometimes, on the warm and sunny days, I sat on the grass under a cherry tree, listening to the baby blue tits cheeping for food.

A few months after Dad died I'd helped Mum to fix a nesting box to the tree trunk. She'd borrowed a ladder from the caretaker and I had stood at the bottom holding the little bag of nails. The blue tits arrived the following spring and they've returned every year since then. If I sat very still on the grass, the parents would fly right over my head with beaks full of fat worms. If it was cold or had been raining, I settled on one of the oak benches and read a book or did a bit of homework.

Once a week I took some flowers, usually lemon-coloured chrysanthemums or, in the spring, daffodils. Yellow was Dad's favourite colour. Every so often, someone else would place flowers on the grave too. They weren't shop-bought like ours, but small, soft posies of garden flowers such as forget-me-nots, pretty pink dahlias or Michaelmas daisies. The blooms were tied together with raffia or a scrap of ribbon and squashed into a jam jar. They appeared every month or two and Mum said they were probably from Dad's cousin Penny. I used to move those flowers slightly to one side, so that mine could take centre stage. When they withered I would chuck the posies away, tucking the jam jar behind the headstone, out of sight. I didn't think that Penny would mind. I knew that she must be a nice person to take the trouble to come and put flowers on Dad's grave, especially after all that time. Mum said that she lived on the other side of London and, although it wasn't that far away, I'd never met her. I'd have liked to because, like me, Dad was an only child and his parents died before I was born, but Mum never seemed to be able to get hold of Penny.

I did hope that one day I'd just bump into her. Those last few weeks in London I really wanted her to turn up, to ask her if she'd keep an eye on the grave for me, make sure it didn't get vandalised or begin to look unloved. One day, as I was sitting on the bench, slightly out of sight of the main gate, I looked up to see a woman walking in my direction. She had swingy brown hair and wore a bright green mac. She held a small bunch of flowers and my heart did a sort of somersault. This was it, I thought. This must be her.

The woman almost stopped walking when she saw me. I smiled. She hesitated, but not as if she was making that split second decision about whether or not to return my smile. Instead I got the impression that she wanted to turn around and hurry back the way she had come. But she picked up her pace and carried on walking straight past, her eyes fixed determinedly straight ahead.

I watched as she picked her way across the grass, the heels of her black patent shoes sinking into the soft turf. She placed the flowers on a really old grave, one with a cracked vase at the base. One that looked as if it hadn't had any visitors for decades. She didn't stop to reflect, just turned, weaving her way in and out of the headstones, avoiding the path in her rush to get to the gate. After she'd gone I went over and looked at those flowers. It was a posy, similar to the ones that sometimes appeared on Dad's grave.

LEAVING

That last night at home I couldn't sleep. I lay awake for hours, sifting through the memories: precious moments with Dad in this house, sitting beside me on the bed, reading a story, his warm impulsive kisses in the middle of my forehead as we snuggled on the sofa together watching *101 Dalmatians*; or all those hours spent in the back garden as he tried to teach me how to balance on my bike without stabilisers. I wasn't sure whether some of them were real memories or things I had made up from stories Mum had told me or mental images from photographs I had seen. But it didn't matter. All that mattered was that Dad had been here with me, in this house, being the perfect father.

"I don't want to leave you, Dad," I whispered into the darkness. "I wish I could take you with me. They do it in films. They have an urn on the mantelpiece containing the ashes of their loved one. Mum could have done that, put you in an urn instead of burying you in the ground – then we could have taken you with us, wherever we went."

I listened hard in case he was trying to answer me. There was nothing. So I held Teddy tightly, pulled my duvet up over my head and tried to block out the future. All I wanted to do was to keep everything I knew and loved close to me, to feel safe. Was that too much to ask?

By the morning I was snappy and clumsy. We'd taken some stuff up to Derbyshire already but there was still quite a lot of stuff to pack up. Twice I nearly dropped a box of precious things on the way to the car. Mum exploded as I caught my flip-flop on the edge of the step and the cardboard box crashed against the door frame. Everything inside made a worrying tinkling noise.

"If you can't be more careful, Laura, then you'd be better off doing something else."

"It's all fine," I said, in a voice that sounded

more reassured than I felt.

"At least put some proper shoes on," she called after me.

"I've packed them all," I called back.

We had the only postman in the world who bothered to close the gate behind him, so I had to balance the box on the brick pillar while I negotiated with the catch. I don't know how it happened but the box toppled over, scraped its way down my shin and landed on my foot with a horrible crash. I didn't have to look inside to know that something, if not everything, must be broken. Mum tore out of the front door.

"For goodness' sake," she yelled. "I told you to be careful."

"I'm sorry." My foot was throbbing and a huge sob gathered momentum in my chest. "It's the gate, I couldn't…"

"Stop! I don't want to hear any excuses."

She looked so hard all of a sudden. Where had my lovely, kind mum gone over these last few months? The box was still resting on my foot, rooting me to the spot.

"The trouble is," I shouted back, "you just don't want to hear anything at the moment, do you?"

I yanked my foot out, intending to make a dramatic exit – except my flip-flop was still stuck. "I'm going for a walk," I said. "You'll be better off without me anyway."

I yanked open the gate and marched out, sharp pieces of gravel embedding themselves in my sole.

"Laura! Come back here!"

I ignored her and carried on walking.

"Laura!" This time it was loud enough to make the neighbours' curtains twitch. "Don't be silly."

I limped on. She caught up with me just before I turned the corner.

"Leave me alone."

My foot was beginning to feel really sore.

"I just thought that you might want this." She thrust the flip-flop in front of my face. "Where are you going?"

"I don't know."

But of course I did and she knew too.

She brushed a strand of hair back from my face. "I'm sorry I shouted."

Tears began to stream down my cheeks. "I'm sorry I dropped the box. Everything will be broken."

She pulled me close. "They're only things, Laura. They're not important."

She clasped me to her. I breathed in her scent: citrus fruit, sunshine, elegance.

"All I want," she murmured, "is for you to be happy."

She pushed me away slightly but held on to the tops of my arms, tilting her head so she could look right into my eyes. "Off you go – don't be too long."

"Don't you want to come?"

She stroked my cheek. "Not this time," she said.

"This is it," I said, crouching by the grave, "time to say goodbye. Can't put it off any longer."

I fingered the frilly petals of some lemon carnations I'd put on the grave the day before.

"I'll come back loads and loads. I won't let your grave become all mossy and neglected like some of them. I'm going to get in touch with Penny to make sure she carries on coming and putting those pretty little posies on your grave. If Mum won't give me her

44

number this time I'll find it somehow. She must have it written down in her diary or something."

The air was so still. Not a leaf moved on the old oak tree. It was the weirdest sensation but it felt as if the whole of the world had stopped for a second. Even my breath seemed to have got stuck in my lungs.

"I really, really don't want to go and live with Gran," I gasped. "If you were around we wouldn't be doing this – not that I want to make you feel guilty or anything like that. It's not your fault you're dead, is it?"

Again I couldn't stop the tears. This time I didn't want to. My fingers splayed against the cool slate headstone, instinctively tracing along the grooves that made up his name:

GARETH JAMES COOPER
BELOVED HUSBAND AND FATHER
VII™ JULY MCMLXXIII - XVIII™ AUGUST MMIV

LOVE IS ETERNAL

I threw my head back; the sky was a blur;

45

saltiness washed back down my throat. "I wish you'd give me some sign," I choked, "let me know that you're here, watching over me, like Mum says."

I held my breath, listened for the slightest clue: the rustle of a leaf, the creak of a branch, the chirp of a bird. Nothing. Absolutely nothing. I shook my head, stood up and shrugged.

"Okay, have it your way, but I promise that I'll be back soon."

And then I left, weaving my way around the graves towards the path. As I passed under the dark, stained lych gate I had the strangest sensation, as if X-ray eyes were boring into my back. I stopped and glanced over my shoulder. The cemetery was deserted.

"You're a bag of nerves, Laura," I said to myself, "or getting 'overwrought' as Gran would say." So I gave myself a little shake and set off for home. Several times I turned to look behind me but there was nothing different to see, no one acting suspiciously. All the same, I couldn't get rid of the feeling that I was being followed.

Derbyshire

That first night at Chestnut Farm I went to bed late. I'd been sitting up in the kitchen, scanning a magazine about some celebs who were living on what seemed to be another planet, rather than in the city I had left only a few hours before.

"Come on, Laura," Mum said, as I tried to make my cocoa last as long as possible. "It's been a long day."

Why didn't I want to go up to that room? There wasn't anything wrong with it. It was Mum's old room, with the same pink rug that had been there when she was growing up but new, bright and breezy Cath Kidston curtains. From the big sash window there was a nice view over the back garden and beyond that, rolling fields dotted with slate-blue dry-stone walls. In the middle of the lawn there was an old well with a little tiled roof. Every summer

Gran would hide the pine cover with pots of bright red and pink geraniums but that July it was bare. To the right of the well stood an old apple tree with a swing attached to one of its gnarled branches. The tree didn't have the strength to produce much of a crop of apples any more but ever since Grandad's father bought the farm in the 1930s there had always been a swing on that tree.

"Laura!"

Mum bolted the back door and gestured to the stairs.

I sighed, unable to put the moment off any longer.

"I'm exhausted," Mum said, stopping on the landing to give me a kiss. "Sleep tight."

"You too," I replied with a little wave as she stepped into her bedroom, out of sight. Suddenly, I felt completely alone, as if everything was absolutely new and strange, which was ridiculous.

Normally, the fact that Gran's bed had moved downstairs to the snug and Mum being at the other end of the corridor wouldn't have bothered me at all, but on that night my breath seemed to snag in my chest and all my senses were on red alert. In my bedroom Mum had set out a few of my bits and pieces to make it feel more like home. It didn't work. They just looked forlorn and displaced and made me feel worse.

It was nearly midnight when I turned out the light and so, so dark. A little owl screeched right outside the window and the stairs creaked as if someone were treading on them. It's just the timbers contracting, I said to myself, just the house settling down for the night. All the same... I couldn't help wondering. Was there someone out there? Had some fugitive hidden in one of the barns and slipped into the house unnoticed? I wanted to get up, to open my door and switch on the landing light for comfort but I daren't. Instead I shuffled down the bed, pulled the covers up high and eventually I think I slept – but not for long and not very deeply.

I awoke with a horrible start. My heart felt as if it wanted to leap out of my chest. My mouth was dry and scratchy. The darkness pressed down on me. I longed for the comfort of street lights filtering through the gap in the curtains or even a faint laser of moonlight. It was quiet, deathly quiet. I was leaning over, trying to find the switch on my bedside lamp, when I heard the noise: the tiniest crackle of metal on metal. I froze. Looked around the room. My eyes were adjusting to the gloom and in the bluish haze I saw my bedroom door opening, very slowly. I tried to reason with myself, to hear sane words rising above the sound of blood pumping through my veins. It was no good. However hard I tried to convince my brain that the door had opened on its own, that the minuscule air current filtering through my slightly open window had tugged at it, it didn't work. Every cell in my body was telling me something different. There was someone there. Someone standing just out of view. Waiting.

"Mum? Is that you?"

I could hardly speak. Silence.

"Gran?"

Stupid to say that. She'd never have made it up the stairs and certainly not without clunking her stick on the steps. The door opened a little more, its hinges making more of that grating sound which I hadn't been able to identify at first.

It was then that I saw him, the shape of a man, standing just inside my room.

I'd sometimes wondered what it would be like to be really terrified, how I'd react. Would I scream and run about, or would I be stuck to the spot? Now I knew. I couldn't move, could barely breathe. It's a cliché, but time really did seem to stop. The man stood completely still. He was tall with broad shoulders but it was too dark to see what he was wearing or make out from his face whether he was someone I knew. It was like a stand-off. Neither of us moved. I was the first to break.

"W-what do you want?"

My voice was little more than a whisper. I could hardly hear it myself. He didn't reply. Shakily, I reached for the light switch again. This time I found it. I swear that I never took my eyes off the man, didn't even blink when light flooded the room. But in an instant he had gone.

LIBERTY

I spent half the night awake, braced in case the man reappeared. Only when dawn broke did I pluck up the courage to get out of bed and scour the house. Everything looked normal. There were no missing pieces of silver or prised open windows so I went back to bed and dropped off to sleep to the sound of birds singing and the clink of bottles in the milk float as it rumbled down the street.

At Gran's everything stops for coffee at eleven o'clock on the dot. I could smell the aroma of freshly ground beans as I trudged down the stairs, preparing myself for an evil look and a tart comment for not surfacing several hours earlier.

"Sleep well?" Mum asked as I entered the kitchen.

"Of course she slept well," Gran butted in. "That's why she's not come down until nearly lunchtime. It's the country air that does it, and the quietness.

None of that constant traffic to keep you awake."

"I like the sound of traffic," I answered back, my resolve not to be annoyed gone in an instant. "Actually I didn't sleep well. I had this really horrible dream. At least I think that's what it was."

"That'll be all those biscuits of mine that you ate after supper," Gran snapped. "Didn't I tell you that no good would come of it?"

Mum shot me a wry smile over the top of Gran's head. "What sort of a dream, sweetheart?"

I half turned away from Gran and directed my answer at Mum. "I thought there was someone in my room. I was positive there was, but when I switched on the light no one was there. I got out of bed later and looked along the landing just to make sure. It was horrible. I was so scared."

Mum came over and put her arm around my shoulders.

"There aren't any ghosts here that no one's told me about, are there?" I asked. "This house isn't haunted?"

Gran snorted into her coffee.

"You are *so* dramatic, Laura – just like your father.

You know that there are no such things as ghosts."

I glared at her. I had no idea what Gran had against my dad but, even after all these years, she grabbed every chance to have a dig at him. It wasn't always what she said. Sometimes it was more what she didn't say. It was the way she raised her eyebrows in an expression of disapproval if his name was mentioned or the fact that she put Mum and Dad's wedding photograph away in a drawer less than a year after he died and never brought it out again. She hated me visiting the grave too.

"It's not healthy," Gran had said, on one of her infrequent visits to London. "And think of all the money you're spending," she'd added, as Mum handed over a five pound note in exchange for a bunch of yellow roses.

I was sure that Gran had been going to say 'wasting' instead of 'spending' but she stopped herself just in time. If she was trying to persuade me that Dad wasn't worth the effort it didn't work. In fact it had just the opposite effect. The more she made her snide remarks the more I took Dad's side.

"There are some things you just know," I said to

Liberty one day when everyone was round at her house and Gran had been having a dig about the way Dad drove too fast. "You don't have to be told them. It's as if they are already inside of you at birth and I know that my dad was the best father in the whole of the universe."

I didn't pick up on the fact that Liberty didn't say much. Besides, I didn't expect her to agree with me. She couldn't remember as much as I could about when we were small and she was bound to think that Uncle Pete was the best dad in the world but I did think she could have said that my dad was second best, just to be nice.

That first morning at Chestnut Farm I helped Mum with a few chores and got out of the house straight after lunch. The sun went behind a cloud as I hurried down Main Street to Liberty's cottage. I shivered and wished I'd picked up my hoodie as I left. A tractor rumbled up the road and Uncle Pete leaned out of the cab and waved. I waved back but could only manage half a smile. Once or twice I thought that I heard steps behind me. I stopped, took off my flip-flops and pretended to dust some grit from the bottom of my feet while quickly glancing back. There were just a couple of elderly ladies chatting in the distance. Nothing to get uptight about.

"It's lack of sleep," I said to myself. "You're imagining things."

All the same I walked to Liberty's as fast as I could without risking looking stupid by breaking into a run.

"Save me!" I shrieked, flinging my arms around her as soon as she opened the front door.

She staggered backwards. Her hair smelled of coconut and was like a ribbon of flaxen silk against my cheek. How I longed for hair like that instead of my tangle of mouse-brown curls.

"Gran's already having a go at me. I need a sanctuary."

She stiffened slightly, not laughing as I expected.

"Uh, okay," she said, not sounding entirely welcoming as she extricated herself from my hug. "So have you totally had enough already then?"

"There's no point whingeing," I replied. "We're here now. Besides, I'm working on my positive thinking…"

I paused, waited for her to groan and say,

"Not again." But she didn't. Instead she just stood there looking stony.

"Are you okay, Lib?" I asked.

"Fine. You didn't text to let me know you were coming."

"Sorry, are you going out?"

"No. I can't. I'm babysitting the boys *again*. I thought that now you were here Mum wouldn't be so tied up and I'd get a bit of time to myself." She sounded really put out and she wasn't looking at me, just using her hair as a shield.

I was a bit thrown for a moment. "I can come back later if you like. I was going to help my mum sort things out but Gran was being a bit awkward and…" I shrugged. "Well, as I said, I can come back later."

Liberty turned on her heel and strode down the dark, quarry-tiled hall.

"You're here now, aren't you?" She called over her shoulder.

I hesitated on the doorstep, wondering whether to follow her or to leave her to stew. Before I could make my mind up a gust of wind hit me hard between the shoulder blades, propelling me straight over the doormat. I crashed into the umbrella stand and was still getting my breath back when the front door slammed closed behind me. Liberty's heart-shaped face appeared around the door frame to the kitchen.

"We've only just had that painted. Mum'll go berserk if it's chipped."

"Sorry," I said. "It was the wind."

"What wind?"

I followed her into the kitchen and looked out of the window. The leaves on the trees were completely still.

"Dunno," I said. "There was this gust. It came from nowhere. It was weird."

Liberty plonked herself down on the sofa and picked up a pot of electric-blue polish from the coffee table. She stroked a slick of blue onto her thumbnail.

"Welcome to Derbyshire," she said. "The weather's different up here. It can be bright sunshine one minute and pouring with rain five minutes later."

"I do know that," I said, laughing. "I have been here before, duh!"

It was an attempt to lighten the atmosphere, which

was still as chilly as those snowbound days they get in the Peak District in winter.

"I suppose you're going to find loads of things are different from now on," she said. There was an edge to her voice that I'd never heard before.

I felt something in my chest, like a trickle of iced water running down behind my breastbone. "What do you mean?"

She didn't look up, just concentrated on covering those long, slender nails with colour. She must have heard the anxiety in my voice. I could hear it as clearly as the church bells that wake me up every Sunday morning in Derbyshire, even after all these years. Liberty flicked her eyelids upwards. It was the briefest of glances, not nearly long enough for me to look into her eyes and try to work out what she was really thinking.

"I just mean that Marshington's really boring compared to London."

"I'm sure I'll cope," I replied. "I'll just have to, won't I? You never know, living here may turn out to be better than I think. At least that's what I'm telling myself."

I waited for her to tell me I was right. She didn't. I've got this really stubborn streak. Gran says that I get it from Dad and she obviously doesn't see it as a quality to be cultivated. Actually I think stubbornness gets a bad name. Sometimes it can be useful. This was one of those times. I didn't want Liberty to make me feel worse and the fact that she was being so negative made me determined to do my best to prove her wrong. I wasn't sure that I'd ever had a light bulb moment before but suddenly my choice was before me, as clear as those crystal decanters on Gran's sideboard. I could spend the next few months or years of my life eaten up with resentment or I could accept the move and make the best of it. If resentment won then I would have let others take control of my life, of my future.

'Sometimes these things happen for the best.' That was one of the things Gran used to say and when I thought that she was referring to Dad it made me really angry, but maybe in this respect she *could* be proved right, I thought. People, especially my old teachers, were always telling me these were meant to be the best years of my life. I didn't want to go through them holding myself back, closing myself down, did

I? It wouldn't be easy, starting at a new school, making new friends, but at least I had Liberty to help. Maybe, just maybe, if I threw myself into everything, this move might not be the third worst thing that had ever happened to me in my entire life after losing Dad and Grandad.

"Besides," I said to Liberty, faking a determination that was still germinating inside of me, "I'm luckier than lots of people, aren't I?"

She raised an eyebrow and twisted her glossed lips, signalling disbelief. I carried on regardless.

"I've got you to help me with things like school. You can introduce me to people and help me to settle in. Loads of people don't have that."

She was very still for a moment, as if weighing up her options.

"No, they don't," she said at last, balancing the bottle of nail polish on the arm of the sofa and holding up one hand for admiration. "We might not be in the same class though."

I perched on the opposite arm.

"Lib, what's wrong? Have I done something to upset you? I thought you'd be pleased that

61

we can spend more time together."

She looked up then, straight at me. I thought she might be about to cry.

"Of course I'm pleased."

The 'but' hung in the air like a giant hoverfly.

"It's just…" she shrugged, "… things have been a bit tense here. My mum and yours haven't exactly been getting on well lately."

"That'll sort itself out," I said. "Besides, just because Mum and Aunt Jane aren't best friends at the moment doesn't mean we have to fall out, does it? It's not a question of taking sides, is it?"

She uncurled, shuffled across the sofa and draped her arms around my neck.

"No, of course not. You're right. You're always right, Laura. I wish I was as sensible as you."

I laughed, felt my spine soften with the relief that she seemed more like herself.

"Yeah right, sensible Laura who was imagining she saw a ghost last night."

"No, really?"

I nodded. Liberty pulled away.

"That's awesome. What did it look like?"

"Scary," I said. "But it was just my brain playing tricks. Some psychologist would say that it's all to do with the move and feeling strange and uprooted."

"Maybe it was Grandad," Liberty said.

"No, it wasn't. Definitely not."

She opened her eyes wide. Questioning.

"I'd have known if it was Grandad. I'd have felt it. Anyway, he wouldn't have wanted to scare me, would he?"

"Of course not," she replied, stroking my arm. "Why are we even talking about this? There are no such things as ghosts. Mind you," she added, "Gran's house is a bit creaky and spooky sometimes."

"Thanks," I said with a wry laugh. "You've made me feel a lot better."

"That's what I'm here for," she replied, looking suddenly serious. "I don't want anything to ever come between us, Laura."

"Then it won't," I said determinedly, and I reached over and screwed the top tightly on the bottle of nail polish, just in case she knocked it over.

Trapped

"You're quiet," Mum said at suppertime.

"Hmm," I replied, toying with the chives sprinkled over my new potatoes.

"Aren't you hungry?"

I shook my head. "Not very."

It had seemed strange walking back from Liberty's house and trying to think of the farm as 'home'. All my positive intentions had disappeared. I just felt fed up and sad, especially as I'd texted Abi and found out that my London friends were all meeting up for a pizza and going to the movies. The last thing I felt like doing was sitting down with Mum and Gran in a kitchen more than a hundred miles away from where I should be.

"That's a waste of good food," Gran said. "In my day—"

"Well it's not your day any more," I said, pushing my chair back and banging it against the front of the dresser, the blue willow-pattern plates tinkling together like a xylophone.

"Laura!" Mum half scolded as I scraped my meal into the bin and clattered the plate into the dishwasher. "What's the matter?"

"It's nothing," I said, brushing past her so fast she didn't have time to put out a hand and catch hold of my arm.

She leaped up. "Wait! It's not nothing. Apologise to your grandmother."

I hesitated, wanted just to ignore her. But it wouldn't be worth the hassle later.

"Sorry," I mumbled, gracelessly throwing the words behind me.

"That's not a proper apology," Mum said, her voice louder and higher pitched.

I bit my bottom lip, took a deep breath and summoned all the self-control I had, ready to apologise again. But just as I turned around and opened my mouth, Gran butted in.

"It's all right, Liz. Let's leave it. It's not worth getting het up about."

Wow! That was a surprise. Mum looked pretty

stunned too as she sank back onto her chair and shot me a look that conveyed in no uncertain terms that I hadn't heard the end of it. But for now, thanks to Gran, I could make my escape.

I was in bed by nine. I turned my light out so Mum wouldn't come in and give me a lecture about everyone making an effort to adjust and the importance of good manners. I heard her come upstairs at about ten-thirty and hesitate outside my door, but she didn't come in. This time as the house made all those weird creaking, groaning noises I didn't feel so bothered. My door was opened wide to allow light from the lamp at the top of the stairs to filter through and Mum knew not to turn it off. It's strange how comforting a little light can be.

I was on the cusp of sleep when something disturbed me. I jolted awake, not sure what had frayed every nerve ending in my body. All I could hear was my heart pounding. My hands gripped the edge of the duvet as my eyes were instinctively drawn towards the door. Every muscle seemed to contract as I saw the silhouette against the landing wall. It was definitely the man again, and he looked taller, broader, stronger than the night before. Slowly he edged into my room and I watched, virtually paralysed, as the door closed behind him. When that last smidgeon of light was snatched away I thought that I might die from fright. My lungs felt completely solid. I could barely breathe in or out. For a few seconds I couldn't see the man at all while my eyes struggled to adjust. But I knew that he was there, shifting the particles of darkness, moving stealthily towards me.

I pulled the duvet up under my chin. It was a warmish night but I felt cold, so cold. My joints were locked. I'd never be able to move fast enough to get away from him and there was no point crying out. Mum and Gran were too far away. No one would hear. The man could smother me before a feeble sound had barely left my mouth. He was getting closer and closer. I was trapped.

SURPRISE

CRASH! Something smashed on the floorboards.
"Damn! Sorry about that."

His voice was deep and vaguely familiar. Now my entire being was like a quivering mass of badly set crème caramel. And people say the countryside is safe, I thought. Only my second night here and I'm about to be murdered in my bed.

"Laura, can you switch the light on? I can't see where I'm going."

Oh my God! He knew my name. How petrifying was that? What was it I'd read about the majority of crimes being committed by someone known to the victim? Was it a person from the village or one of the men who worked for Uncle Pete on the farm?

"W-what do you want?" How I managed those words I had no idea.

"I want to talk to you."

Yeah right! I thought. That's why people break into fourteen-year-old girls' bedrooms in the middle of the night, just to talk.

"Please, Laura," he repeated, "switch the blessed light on. I'm meant to be able to see in the dark but this is all a bit new to me and quite frankly everything's a bit of a blur."

He certainly didn't sound like your average homicidal maniac. In fact, I was beginning to think that he sounded a bit nervous, which was unexpected. After all, he had the upper hand. I bit my lip hard and reached for the lamp. As the light lit up the room I blinked, shielding my eyes for a second. I didn't see him straight away. The first thing I saw as I scanned the room was my china goose, a present from Liberty, smashed to smithereens on the floorboards.

"I hope it wasn't too precious. I don't think it can be glued."

I looked in the direction of the voice and there he was, standing in front of the dressing table.

"Surprise!" he said, throwing his arms up and out to the side and nearly sending a little blue vase flying through the air. Then, "Oops!" as he cupped his hands around it in the nick of time.

I actually rubbed my eyes. They do that in films and I always thought it was over the top, but I realised that when you've got something so unexpected, so unbelievable in front of you, it's a natural reaction.

He moved towards me. I recoiled.

"Uh oh," he sighed. "You're upset. I thought this might happen. I did wonder if I should have made a more gradual entrance, taken a few weeks rather than a few hours, but at the end of the day, that's not really my style. I'm too impatient for that softly, softly approach. I did try to break you in gently with a semi-appearance last night but it obviously didn't work. You look petrified, which is not what I wanted at all."

I couldn't answer him, couldn't get my head around what was happening to me. The man took a couple of steps closer, the hint of a frown crossing his face.

"Laura, you *do* know who I am, don't you?"

I managed a tiny tip of my head. Yes, of course I knew who he was. All those years of wondering if Mum was right when she said that he was watching over me. All those years of wondering if he would ever come back to see me. All those years of wondering if the thoughts that went around and around in my head made me a bit of a mental case. And yet, impossible as it seemed, there he was, standing in my bedroom, dressed in jeans and a blue and white checked shirt and looking almost human. My dad.

"Oh dear! Can you speak? I haven't caused you to lose your voice? Shock can do that sometimes, can't it?" He peered at me in a worried way.

"No, it's okay."

Was that raspy sound coming from my mouth really my voice?

"I'm okay."

I didn't mean it. I was about as far from okay as I'd ever been.

He clasped his hands to his chest and sighed. "Excellent! I knew you wouldn't be a wimp." Another frown. His whole face rippled when he did that. "You don't look very pleased to see me though."

I shook my head. "I-I just can't believe it, that's all," I stammered. "Are you real? Am I imagining you? Is this all a dream?"

"Don't I look real?" he asked, a bit indignantly. "I'm as real as you are!"

He touched his hands to his shoulders and wafted them down his front. As he did so his whole form rippled apart like lots of little trails through soapy water, before melding back together again.

"Hmm!" he murmured. "Maybe you're right. I can see this body issue might be a bit of a problem for you to take on board. Have you done the molecule thing at school?"

He didn't wait for me to respond.

"Well, you know that protons, electrons and neutrons combine to form atoms, which are the building blocks of molecules?"

"Sort of," I mumbled.

"Then the molecules combine to form chemicals, which are what the cells of the body are made of. Following that, the cells combine to form tissues and the tissues combine to form organs, and so on and so on, blah, blah, blah, and hey presto you have a human."

My head was spinning now. What was this? Some nightmare of a physics lesson? Or just simply a nightmare?

"Yes, I know all of that," I replied, "but you're *not* human, are you? You're not solid matter and you're sort of glowing around the edge."

He looked down at himself and grinned. "So I am. I don't know how that's happened. Cool though, isn't it? Anyway, to answer your previous questions – no, you are not imagining me, and I am most definitely not a dream *or* a nightmare. At least I hope you don't think it's a nightmare because here I am, large as life." He paused. "Well not that large. I do try to keep trim and the life thing's a bit inaccurate, but you get what I mean."

"So," I said, slowly, "you're a ghost?"

He threw his arms upwards and a waft of air lifted all of my clothes off the big, squashy chair underneath the window and deposited them in a heap in the middle of the floor.

"I do hate that word," Dad said. "It has such negative connotations."

"How *would* you describe yourself then?" I asked.

He stood up tall, squared his shoulders.

"I'm not that different to you," he said proudly.

73

"I am a cloud of molecules."

"Oh!" I replied. "I see. That explains everything."

"I knew that you'd understand," he said. "I told everyone on The Other Side that my Laura's as clever as anything."

Actually I'm not clever at all, well, not nearly as clever as Liberty, and I couldn't get my head around the molecule thing, but it seemed cruel to dash his hopes of fathering a child genius at this early stage in the renewal of our relationship.

"What I don't understand," I said, beginning to relax and hugging my knees underneath the duvet, "is why you are here. Why now, after all this time?"

"You sounded upset," he replied. "And between you and me..." he looked around conspiratorially, dropped his voice to a whisper, "... I'd be pretty distraught too, having to move in with the old battleaxe. What your mother is thinking of, I really don't know."

He puffed out his chest and carefully raised both hands, palms facing outwards.

"So I came to see if I could help."

He probably wanted some sort of thanks but

I was too shell-shocked to remember my manners. "You *were* listening to me, when I talked to you?" I gasped.

"Of course, all the time. I know everything about you."

That was a bit disconcerting.

"Everything?"

His grin broadened. "Pretty much."

A little flare of anger kindled in my chest. "Then why didn't you let me know before that you were there?"

His face fell. The glowing light around his edge shivered, as if he was upset. "I wanted to." His voice was so low I had to lean forwards to hear him. "I wanted to come back and say sorry for making such a mess of things."

He sank onto the dressing table stool, bent forwards and covered his face with his hands for a moment, the ends of his long, pale fingers resting in his hair. Hair that was just like mine.

"But I wasn't sure whether you would want to see me. I didn't want to make things worse."

"How could you have made things any

worse?" I snapped back, unable to help myself. "If you were *really* listening to me then you'd know how much I longed for some sign. I wanted that more than anything. I've been looking for you, listening for you everywhere, almost every single day since you… left."

He bit his lip and put one hand to his chest.

"I was listening, Laura. I promise. But sometimes we think we want something and then, when we get it, it's not what we wanted at all."

He was talking in complete riddles. I blinked. Sudden tears clung to my eyelashes. My vision went all blurry.

"No, you're wrong," I said. "You *were* wrong to think that. If I could have seen you or heard you, if I could have known that you *were* still there watching over me, I'd have felt…"

What would I have felt? Protected? More complete? Happier? Probably all of those things. How could he have denied me that? How could he not have known what a difference it would make?

"I'm sorry," he said. "I didn't want to complicate things. You seemed to be doing okay. I just wanted

76

what was best for you."

I wiped tears from my cheeks with the back of my hand.

"But I wanted to be better than okay," I muttered. "Whatever I did, however much I tried, there's always been this piece of me that's missing."

"And that's my fault," he said. "I know that."

He looked as if he was about to cry too.

"The accident wasn't your fault," I sniffed.

"I don't blame you for that. I just wish you'd come back sooner."

"Well I'm here now, my princess."

I wanted him to hug me but he stayed sitting on the stool. "And now we can make up for all of that lost time. We can get to know each other properly, can't we?"

My eyes widened. "You mean you're staying?"

"Oh yes, most definitely," he said, a grin flashing across his face. "Now that I'm here, I'm not leaving you."

QUESTIONS

Along the corridor a door creaked. I heard the pad of slippers on the carpet that ran along the centre of the landing. Dad leaped off the stool and made a dash for the corner of the room.

"Laura!" Mum opened the door and stepped inside. "Are you all right? I thought I heard voices. Why is your light on? Can't you sleep?"

She sniffed the air.

"What's that smell? It reminds me of…"

She shook her head.

"No, it can't be."

"What smell, Mum?"

She frowned.

"I just got a whiff of something. It smelled like your father's favourite aftershave."

She shivered.

"Silly me. I'm imagining things."

She stared at the pile of clothes in the middle of the floor. I expected her to say something but she looked distracted as she bent down and picked them up, draping everything back onto the chair. Then she spotted the goose.

"Oh dear, what's happened here?" I glanced at Dad, who appeared to be frantically trying to fade and not making a particularly good job of it from what I could see.

"I-I got up to go to the toilet and knocked it off."

"Who were you talking to?"

I paused, wondering whether to tell her the truth but Dad was making panic-stricken gestures and mouthing, "No, no, no," over and over again.

"No one," I said, thinking that I sounded totally unconvincing. "I was probably saying things in my sleep."

"You've never done that before," Mum replied, bending down. "It must be all the stress."

Tentatively she picked up the broken goose.

"Oh dear. You *have* made a mess of this. I think it's beyond repair."

As she turned and walked towards the corner

to drop the pieces in the bin, Dad flattened himself against the wall with a look of alarm on his face. Surely she would see him and for some peculiar reason he didn't want her to.

"MUM! STOP!"

She turned back towards me and a little whoosh of relief filled the room as Dad wiped a hand theatrically across his forehead.

"Can you put the goose here?" I patted my bedside table. "Liberty gave it to me so it's special. I don't just want to chuck it. I'll look at it in the morning."

She dropped the broken china onto a tissue and placed it next to me.

"Brr!" she said, shivering and pulling her dressing gown around her. "This room is so cold tonight. I can't think why. It's quite warm outside. Do you want a hot-water bottle?"

I lay back down, suddenly desperate to get rid of her, desperate to get Dad to myself before he disappeared into thin air.

"No, I'm good, thanks."

She stroked my cheek.

"You do look pale. I hope you're not coming down

with something."

She leaned over to kiss me.

"It's going to be all right, Laura, us living here, isn't it?"

I looked up into her soft, hazel eyes.

"Yes, Mum. I'm sure it's going to be fine."

"I don't want you to feel that you're missing out on loads of excitement."

I looked over her shoulder, towards Dad.

"Don't worry, Mum," I said, faking a yawn and half closing my eyes. "I'm sure there'll be loads of exciting things happening. Just not quite what I'm used to."

"Phew!" Dad murmured when she had gone. "That was a close call."

I sat up in bed. He moved away from the corner, and shook himself as if to relieve some tension.

"She couldn't see you, could she?" I whispered.

"No, thank goodness. I wasn't sure if she'd be able to or not."

"It's a pity. She'd have loved it. I'm sure she would."

"Hmm, maybe."

"So why couldn't she see you and I can?"

He shrugged. "I don't know. Maybe it's to do with heightened sensitivity and expectations. As you said, you've been looking for me for a long time. You wanted to see me."

"Do you think that you could make her see you?"

"Possibly, if I really wanted her to and she was open to it."

"Why don't we try it? Why don't I point you out to her next time?"

"No!"

His tone was quite sharp. He began to pace up and down the room.

"No." His voice was softer now but he was frowning. "You mustn't tell your mother about me, Laura. It must be our secret. Do you understand?"

He came to an abrupt standstill, staring at me, waiting for my answer. I wondered if our future depended upon what I said next. If I said no, would he disappear? I felt empty and weak at the thought of it, the way you feel when you've been ill and haven't eaten for a couple of days. So, although I didn't understand, I nodded, pretended that I did. "If that's what you want."

"It is. And I can't tell you anything about my life on The Other Side. So you mustn't ask."

Suddenly uncertainty, maybe even distrust, hovered around his eyes.

"I just want you to stay," I whispered. "Please. I won't tell Mum about you. I won't ask any awkward questions. I promise."

He visibly relaxed and smiled. "That's my princess."

I beamed at his praise and the hollow space inside of me was filled with happiness. He chucked my clothes on the floor again and arranged himself on the big, squashy chair. It was strange to watch, like seeing particles of dust dancing in sunlight or a swarm of bees swirling and whirling. "I'm going to make myself nice and comfy," he said, "and I can watch over you all night long. Your mum used to do that when you were little and running a temperature. She'd camp at the side of your bed. Well, it's my turn now."

"But I'm not tired. There are so many things I want to ask you."

"It's late, Laura, and you always did need your sleep or you were very ratty in the morning."

"That was then and this is now," I protested.

But a yawn suddenly expanded inside of me. I tried to stop it by taking a sip of water. So many questions were jostling for attention inside my head. My brain felt like one of those candyfloss machines you see at the fair but this time the sugary strands were my thoughts whizzing around and around, increasing in volume until I thought my head would burst from the pressure. The yawn couldn't be resisted either. I put my hand to my mouth to try to hide it. He leaned forwards in the chair.

"I'll still be here in the morning, Laura. We've got plenty of time to catch up." He placed a hand to his chest. "I promise."

I lay down and closed my eyes.

"Dad?"

"Yes?"

"Was that you at Liberty's house, pushing me through the front door? Were you that funny gust of wind?"

"You couldn't seem to make your mind up so

84

I thought I'd decide for you."

"And when I left the cemetery, before we came to Marshington, I felt that someone was following me. Was that you too?"

"Uh huh!" he sighed.

"Have you been with me ever since that day?"

"Most of the time."

"That's nice."

"Good. Go to sleep now."

"One more question."

"What?"

I wondered if I detected a hint of irritation in that response. Perhaps he expected me to do exactly as I was told, as if I were still four years old. "How long *are* you staying for?"

He didn't answer for a moment. I shifted onto one elbow so I could see him better. He looked straight at me.

"For as long as you need me, Laura. That's how long I'll stay."

"I'll need you for ever," I whispered.

He just smiled. I wanted to get up, to touch him, to see what he felt like, if he felt of anything at all, but I was afraid that if I did he might disappear so I settled down again in my bed, closed my eyes and tried to take in everything that had happened. It was the stuff of dreams. In a matter of minutes I had changed. I felt different. My daddy had come back to be here, with me, and if that could happen, anything seemed possible.

DISCOVERY

My eyes flipped open. Daylight flooded through the curtains. I looked at the chair. It was empty. I couldn't believe it. He had broken his promise! He had gone.

"Dad? Are you there?"

No reply, no misty shape standing on my carpet. So he had lied. Surely you'd be penalised for that in the afterlife? Weren't you meant to be free of all those human vices like telling porky pies? Wasn't your soul meant to be pure or was that all a myth and in fact you were just like you were in your land-locked days? Except Dad hadn't been a liar, had he?

I flopped back against my pillow, a tightness in my throat. Perhaps I'd imagined it all. The events of the previous night spooled through my brain like a YouTube video and suddenly to think that he had been here, talking to me, seemed utterly ridiculous. But he *had* seemed so real and the disappointment that I felt searing through every cell in my body was definitely for real. I didn't even try to stop myself from crying.

"Don't be so stupid," I said to myself, reaching for a tissue, my hand brushing the broken goose, which lay in pieces on my bedside table where Mum had left it. That goose looked at me with its beady eyes.

So, it seemed to be saying, *not so sure now, are you? But if it didn't all happen as you originally thought, how did I get broken?*

"You fell off the shelf," I said out loud to the goose. "It's a funny house, sloping walls, sloping floors. You were too near the edge and you slipped. End of."

The goose stared back, disbelievingly.

"Oh for goodness' sake," I muttered. "I've been here for less than a day and I really am going completely mad."

By the time I'd washed, dressed and not even bothered to double-check in the mirror for those spots that sprout in the night like evil little toadstools, I'd convinced myself that it was all a dream. A stupid, energy-sapping, emotion-churning dream and I hated it. I never, ever wanted to have a dream like that again, to be left feeling so cheated, so completely flattened. The grandfather clock in the hall chimed quarter past eleven as I trudged down the stairs, ready to endure one of Gran's withering looks. She was sitting at the kitchen table, cheeks sucked in, lips pursed. She lifted her wrist and threw a meaningful look at Grandad's old watch.

"Don't start," I muttered under my breath. "I'm really not in the mood."

Then I stopped. My mouth fell open. Oh my God! It hadn't been a dream. He hadn't abandoned me. Dad was there, sitting at the table right next to Gran, and while she looked disapprovingly at me, he ladled four spoonfuls of sugar into her coffee. He mouthed, "Good morning," and with his free hand gave me a little wave.

"What are you gawping at?" Gran snapped.

She had no idea what was going on. Like Mum she obviously couldn't see him.

"Nothing," I said. "It's just such a beautiful day, isn't it? I'm so happy."

"I suppose it is if you can get out and about," Gran retorted, picking up her mug with a slightly shaky hand. "And happiness doesn't last long, in my opinion."

I pressed my lips together and watched as she drank some coffee.

"Ugh!" Gran almost spat a mouthful of hot liquid over the blue checked tablecloth.

Dad got up from his chair and stood next to the window, shivering with laughter.

"What have you done to this coffee?" she demanded as Mum emerged from the pantry. "It tastes like syrup."

"I haven't done anything. It's the same as normal."

"It's not."

Dad was doubled up now. He was shaking so much I'm surprised the tablecloth didn't blow off the table, taking the crockery and fruit bowl with it. I was trying my best not to laugh too.

"Perhaps you forgot how much sugar you'd put in," Mum said gently. "It's easily done."

"It's my hip that's not healing, not my brain," Gran snapped. "I know exactly how much sugar

I added." She glared at me. "I don't know what you're smiling at, young lady. Is this your doing?"

"Mother, really! Laura's only just walked into the room. That's a bit uncalled for."

I didn't hold my breath for an apology but Gran did look slightly shamefaced as she pushed the mug away.

"You know I like a cup and saucer, Liz. Even without all that sugar it wouldn't taste the same in a mug."

Mum whisked the mug away and surreptitiously raised her eyebrows at me.

"You're looking better," she said to me. "What do you fancy for breakfast?"

"Breakfast!" Gran chuntered. "She might as well wait for lunch."

Dad had started doing a mean impression of Gran in full rant. I grabbed a packet of cereal from the pantry and frowned at him. How was I meant to pour my cornflakes into the bowl without spilling them, let alone eat in a civilised manner, with him doing a stand-up comedy routine in the background? Mum put another coffee in front of Gran, this time in a delicate bone china cup and saucer. I leaned over and deliberately moved the sugar bowl towards me so Dad couldn't reach it. His bottom lip did an overly dramatic pout. I returned his expression with a headmistressy one of my own. As I ate and he paced the kitchen, running his fingers over various objects, I couldn't eat my cereal quickly enough. I wanted to get us both out of there so that I could have him all to myself.

"She hasn't changed," Dad said as we walked down the village street. "She's still the same grumpy old biddy."

"I've already sussed that you two didn't get on," I replied.

"That's a bit of an understatement," he chuckled, "not that I didn't try."

Involuntarily I twisted my lips. "Really? That's not what *she* says."

He stopped, put his hand to his heart area. "Of course I tried, Laura. How can you possibly think otherwise?"

He fell into step beside me again and I felt a warmth creep through me, despite the fact we were walking on the shady side of the street. This was what it was like, walking with your dad, talking with your dad. Such simple things, something loads of people took for granted every day, but for me it was something I'd always dreamed of, something I'd believed would never happen. I'd often watched my friends and their fathers strolling down the street, chatting, laughing, teasing, leaning in towards each other, totally absorbed and at ease in each other's company. Even when they looked embarrassed or rolled their eyes because of something their dads had done or said I'd wanted to know what it felt like. Now I knew just what it was like having your dad right next to you and it was one of the best feelings I'd ever had. I wanted to bottle it and put it on my dressing table in one of those pretty enamel-topped scent bottles that Gran collected.

"The trouble was," Dad continued, "your grandmother never thought that I was good enough."

"Doesn't every mother think that about their daughter's husband or boyfriend?" I asked. "She probably wasn't that keen on Uncle Pete either, to begin with."

He shrugged. "Maybe you're right but I wouldn't be like that with you."

"I bet you would."

"No, I wouldn't. Have you got a boyfriend?"

I tilted my head, looked up at him. "Don't you know? I thought you knew everything about me."

For a moment he seemed lost for words.

"You're too young for boyfriends anyway," he said. "You want to concentrate on your school work so you can get a good job. That's the way forward in your world, Laura – education."

Now he was beginning to sound like a politician.

"It's a shame your gran didn't make me more welcome," he said, a touch wistfully as he gazed at the stone houses with their slate roofs and hollyhock-filled front gardens. "I actually liked coming here but *she* always managed to spoil it."

"At least you were only here for a few days at a time," I said. "I'm trying to put on a brave face for Mum's sake but to be honest it's going to be a nightmare actually living with Gran. I *would* like

Mum to find a house for just the two of us as soon as possible."

"I'll see what I can do," he said with a grin.

"What do you mean?"

"I'm sure I can help things along. That's what I'm here for, to help."

I stopped, leaned against a low stone wall and looked at him. He looked just the same as he did in the last photo taken of us together at the fair. He was tall, slim, good-looking and didn't look old enough to be the dad of a fourteen year old.

"I still can't believe that you're really here," I said. "But I am glad, very glad."

I wanted to put my arms around him, to feel what it was like to have a hug from him, but I held back and he didn't make the first move. Suddenly there was a touch of awkwardness between us.

"I'm glad that I'm here too," he said softly. "We're going to have a lot of fun together."

He smiled and the tension dissolved.

"I can feel it in my bones."

"You don't have any bones," I said with a laugh.

"So I don't! Well, I can feel it in my aura then."

95

His edges shimmered with white mist but amongst it there were other colours, if you looked closely: patches of pale purple, specks of yellow, tadpole squiggles of green. As I watched, the mistiness expanded and reached towards me. I took a step backwards.

"Hey! What's happening?" I asked, fear stabbing at my stomach.

"It's fine, Laura," he said. "Don't worry. It's like a virtual hug."

"Oh!" I replied and stayed where I was, let the mist reach me. I'd expected it to be cold and damp but it was warm and soft as it touched my bare arms and legs and swirled up towards my face.

"This is nice," I said, "but I'd rather have a real hug."

"This is almost as good as a real hug," Dad said.

Almost. It's one of those words which reeks of disappointment but the mist did feel soft and comforting. I closed my eyes and imagined a million tiny airborne kisses swirling around me. If I tilted my head to one side I could almost believe that Dad's cheek was resting against mine. "It's not quite the same though, is it?" I said, opening my eyes.

Suddenly he looked really sad, as if he was about to cry. He shook his head.

"No. I'm sorry. It's not. I daren't give you a real hug. I don't know what will happen, whether it's safe." I reached out instinctively and almost touched him. He jumped away.

"It doesn't matter," I said, letting my arms slump to my sides. But of course it did matter and tears filled the corners of my eyes. Suddenly the virtual hug was too much, the mist was too dense, too claustrophobic, and yet at the same time it wasn't enough. My head was full of confusion and then a sort of tidal wave of dizziness seemed to sweep across my brain. I staggered, felt my knees begin to buckle and caught hold of the gatepost leading into the churchyard in the nick of time.

"Laura, are you all right?" Dad asked.

He was so close to me now I could have just put out my hand and touched him.

"I'm sorry. I upset you."

I lifted my head slowly, dug my fingers into the stonework, feeling loose, gravelly chippings and a little mound of moss beneath my skin. Over the top of the wall an auburn-haired boy was straightening up, shears in one hand, clipped grass scattered over his trainers. "Are you okay?" he called.

"Yes, fine," I called with a slightly disembodied voice. "Just tripped, that's all."

I felt like such a fool. He walked towards me.

"You sure you're okay?"

I nodded, sensed Dad getting edgy by my side. The boy didn't appear to be able to see him. His eyes were totally fixed on me and I felt myself blush. It must have been absolutely blaring out of my face, my neck, my chest, even spreading up into the roots of my hair.

"It's easily done," the boy said. "These pavements are full of potholes. I've almost gone flying myself once or twice." He had freckles and a smile that was so open it was disconcerting. Suddenly I was completely tongue-tied and I had no idea why. Boys didn't usually have this effect on me. "Are you new here?"

"Yes," I replied.

It was all I could manage.

Something began tugging at my elbow. It was

as if I had a lasso around my arm, pulling me backwards. I didn't have to look around to know it was Dad.

"I've got to go," I said. "Sorry."

"What's your name?" the boy asked.

"Laura."

"Hi, Laura." His smile broadened and a dimple appeared at the bottom of his right cheek. It looked really cute. "Maybe I'll see you around."

Was it a question or a statement? I wasn't sure. All the time I was backing away, being reeled in like some disobedient animal.

"Yeah," I replied. "Maybe."

I meant to sound cool but it just came out as unfriendly.

"Aargh!" I groaned when we were out of sight. "I sounded like an idiot and he was really nice."

"Do you think so?" Dad asked, with a frown rippling his forehead. "I'm not sure I like the look of him."

"Is that why you dragged me away?" I asked, shaking my arm and trying to free myself from the thread which I could now see was wound around my wrist like one of those toddler straps or a dog lead.

"You shouldn't go talking to strangers," he replied. "In fact, the more I think about it, the more suspect he seems."

"No he doesn't. He looks perfectly normal. He might even be at the school I'm going to in September. Besides, he was working in the churchyard so surely he can't be that bad?"

Dad frowned. "Hmm," he responded. "When I was young, teenage boys didn't hang around graveyards, clipping grass. He's bound to be up to no good. The minute we've gone he'll probably be ripping the lead off the porch roof or breaking in at the back of the church and stealing the silver. It's a good thing I'm here to protect you from people like that, Laura."

I flashed him a glance to see if he was joking but he looked deadly serious.

"I can protect myself thanks very much," I replied. "Okay, I admit that it's a bit strange he was in the churchyard but that doesn't mean he's a complete weirdo."

Dad shook his head as if I was completely deluded. "You never can tell. People aren't always what they seem, you know."

"I know. I'm not stupid. What about ghosts?" I asked, in an attempt to jolt him out of overprotective mode. "Are they always what they seem to be?"

I peered at him, stifled a giggle, waited for his face to break into a smile, but it didn't happen. Obviously I had to try harder.

"Hang on a moment, maybe you're not my dad after all. Maybe you're an imposter in a ghostly dadlike disguise. Maybe I don't know you at all and you have some deep, dark secret buried deeply in your past."

He looked shocked, upset even.

"You don't really think that?"

"No, of course I don't," I laughed. "I'm only joking."

"Phew!" he said, with a wobbly grin and an exaggerated sweep of his hand, but just for a second or two, for some reason, I'd definitely had him worried.

TENSION

Liberty was busy for the next couple of days but to be honest I didn't mind. In fact, secretly I was quite pleased because I wanted to spend the time with Dad. And obviously he wanted to be with me, which was lovely, but there are times a girl needs a bit of privacy.

"Dad, I'm going to the toilet," I hissed as he followed me into the cloakroom during our first day together. "You don't have to hold my hand any more. I'm not scared that a rat is going to appear from the U-bend or I'm going to fall down and be flushed away!"

I thought he'd got the message but then that night he stood by the bathroom door.

"What are you doing?" I asked.

"Just checking that you're all right," he replied.

"I'm fine," I said. "I'm going for a bath."

"You won't nod off and slip under the water will

you?" he fretted.

"Uh no," I said. "I've never done that before."
I waved my book at him. "This should keep me
awake."

Big mistake. I knew it as soon as he peered at
the cover which had a boy and girl in a hot clinch.

"Laura!" He looked genuinely shocked. "I don't
think that's suitable reading."

He made a swift movement as if to grab the
book from me. But I was quicker. I whisked it
behind my back.

"It's perfectly all right," I replied, making a
wafting movement with my hands in order to get
him to step back across the threshold.

"It doesn't look it."

"No," I said slowly, trying to be serious,
"but appearances can be deceptive. All the girls
keep their clothes on and the boys are perfect
gentlemen."

"Hmm," he said in a disbelieving way.

He took a step back onto the landing and
I thought for a moment that I'd placated him. "But
what if you feel dizzy again?" he persisted. "You

might fall and knock your head and…"

Time to get tough.

"Dad," I said firmly. "Stop worrying. I'll be fine."

His shoulders slumped. "If you're sure?"

"I am. Go and… I don't know… do whatever ghosts do when they've got some spare time."

I closed the door and slid the bolt across. It was actually nice to have a bit of space.

There was a light knock on the door.

"What now?"

"You will remember to brush your teeth?"

I smiled and shook my head.

"Yes, Dad, I'll remember. I've managed without you for the last ten years and my teeth haven't gone black and fallen out yet."

"Point taken," he murmured.

At last he was quiet.

The trouble was that Dad seemed to think I was still the same person he'd left behind all those years ago. He still thought of me as four years old and needing to be looked after. Some things were the same of course. I still hated drinking orange squash and eating cheese and onion crisps together because it made me feel sick, and big, hairy spiders still made me shriek until I shook. But in other ways I was a totally different person. Sometimes I wondered what I would have been like if Dad had lived. Would that free-spirited little girl in the photographs have grown up differently? Would I have felt more confident, less worried that everything precious would be taken away from me if I wasn't good and didn't keep my room tidy and work hard at school? I wished I could be more like her, the four year old with the wispy blond hair and carefree smile.

"You want to lighten up a bit," Gran used to say. "Plenty of time to be all orderly when you're old."

"I'm fine as I am thanks," I'd reply.

Except, deep down, I wasn't sure that was true. Part of me was missing. There had been this silent space in my life which made me unsure of who I really was. Now that Dad was back I had a chance to fill that gap and find the real me.

On my second afternoon with Dad, when Gran had gone for her rest, we lolled about in the garden. Dad sat beside me on the swing seat and told me stories about things we'd done together when I was little. "Do you remember when we took a rowing boat out on that little boating lake in the park near home and your mother was rowing but she dropped an oar in the water?"

I shook my head.

"You must have been about three at the time. She told me to leave it, that we could manage with one, but I didn't take any notice, as usual. I leaned over and fell in."

"I bet that was funny," I giggled.

"Your mother didn't think so. She said the whole boat nearly capsized but the lake wasn't deep so I could have scooped you up and carried you to the shore. Not that Mum saw it like that. She wouldn't talk to me for the rest of the day, called me 'irresponsible'."

I pulled a face.

"She didn't like me taking you near water after that. I had a real job to persuade her to let me take you back to feed the ducks. 'Promise me you won't take her in a boat,' she used to say, every single time."

At the base of my spine, something tingled and

in my head a distant memory twisted out of the recesses.

"I remember us going to see the ducklings," I said. "I remember you holding my hand. I had red woolly gloves because it was still cold and afterwards we sat and ate pancakes at a little café."

"Yes," he said, clapping his hands, making the molecules twist and dance up in the air. "Yes, that's right. You always had that chocolate spread and I had maple syrup. Fancy you remembering that."

I felt so pleased with myself and Dad was obviously thrilled too. He was jigging about and rocking the swing seat backwards and forwards.

"And I remember sitting on your shoulders as we walked home," I said and I turned towards him, my eyes widening. "And I remember just how I felt, how much I loved being up there. I felt so special, as if I was the King of the Castle with my own special view of the world. You clutched at the front of my legs and I curled my fingers around your hair. You used to cut across the grass instead of taking the path across the park and you had to keep ducking to avoid the low branches of the trees bashing me on the head."

"Yes, that's right," Dad said. "What about the fair? Do you remember going to that?"

I frowned and tried my best. There was fairground music filling my ears and bright lights and swirling colours soaking my senses but this time there was no Dad in the picture.

"You loved the teacups," he said. "We would whizz around so fast and Mum would close her eyes and tell the man to stop spinning. But you and I would say, 'More, more.'"

"Urgh!" I said. "I hate those teacups now. I was sick in one once. Now just looking at them makes me feel queasy."

"That's right," Dad replied. "You *were* sick, all over Mum's new jeans. I'd forgotten that. Goodness me, she was cross. You know what she's like about her clothes."

We both laughed out loud just as Mum walked into the garden to get the washing off the line.

"Someone sounds happy," she called over.

I glanced at Dad, put my finger to my lips.

"It's just something I was reading," I replied,

thankful that she couldn't see the book on my lap wasn't actually open.

"Maybe I can borrow it after you've finished," Mum said, folding the clothes neatly into the wicker basket. "I could do with a bit of light relief."

Teamwork

Gran was being difficult with Mum. Whatever she did it wasn't quite right and Mum's face had taken on the flat expression of someone who is biting back home truths. Aunt Jane wasn't helping. She kept dropping by and every time it felt as if she was checking up on us or even trying to stir up trouble.

"Are you all right, Mother?" she asked Gran, in a voice overloaded with sympathy.

"Yes, why wouldn't I be?" Gran replied.

I almost liked Gran for that response. I'd expected her to complain as usual.

"Well, you know," Aunt Jane said, with a conspiratorial smile, "is Liz looking after you properly?"

Gran's eyes narrowed. She fingered the small gold cross that she always wore around her neck.

"Of course she is. I'm being looked after very well, thank you, dear."

Why did I think that Aunt Jane was hoping she would say something different?

"Oh, good," she replied in an unconvincing way.

You'd think my aunt would have been happy that we were there at last, taking some of the pressure off her, but she couldn't resist making out that we weren't quite doing things as well as she would have done.

"Mother likes the marmalade put in the Wedgwood pot instead of left in the jar," she'd say. Or, "Mother likes a flat sheet on the bed, not a fitted one, and don't forget to do proper hospital corners. You do know how to do those, don't you, Liz?"

On our third night Aunt Jane popped in just as supper was being served.

"Mother won't like you serving the vegetables straight from the pan, Liz," Aunt Jane whispered in Mum's ear, "and she likes the table to be set properly."

Mum nearly boiled over alongside the peas at that point. I saw her cheeks flush and her pupils dilate. She clattered a saucepan lid down on the work surface and splatted some mashed potato straight onto the plate.

"Like yours, you mean?" she snapped. "I mean your table could be photographed for a magazine, couldn't it, Jane?"

I stifled a smile.

"What's the matter?" Gran asked, putting her crossword book down on the table. "Are you two arguing?"

"No," Mum replied. "It's nothing."

Gran looked pale, her hands trembling slightly as she tried to stop the pen rolling onto the floor. "I don't want any upset. Not because of me."

Dad was sitting in the corner and raised his eyebrows. I frowned at him.

"Don't worry, Gran," I said, taking the pen and wedging it next to the fruit bowl in the middle of the table. "Everything's fine."

She pulled her cardigan closer, looked up at me as if seeking reassurance. For a brief moment I almost felt sorry for her.

"I do hope so, Laura," she murmured. "I really do."

It wasn't fine though. There was this atmosphere whenever Aunt Jane was around and Dad wasn't helping either. On the third night after he'd made his appearance, when everyone was asleep, Dad took his and Mum's wedding photograph out of the desk drawer and placed it on Gran's bedside table, right next to her bed.

It must have been the first thing she saw when she woke up. She shouted so loudly I'm surprised that she didn't wake the whole village.

"Liz, Liz, come here quickly!"

I checked my clock: 4.27 a.m. Dad was curled up in his usual place. Why did I get the impression that he was only pretending to be asleep?

"What on earth is that row?" he asked, stretching and yawning.

"It's Gran," I replied.

"What's got into the old bat now?"

"I don't know but I do wish you wouldn't talk about her like that."

I flew downstairs to see an ashen-faced

Mum flinging open the door to Gran's room.

"What is it? What's the matter?"

"This!" Gran pointed at the photograph. "Who put that there?"

Mum raked her hair back from her face, clasped her hand to her chest.

"I don't know. Is that it? Is that what all the commotion was about?" Mum was shaking. "I thought something awful had happened."

Even my heart was hammering but then I spotted Dad in the hall, grinning from ear to ear.

"What have you been up to?" I mouthed. "Was that you?"

He slapped a hand over his mouth but it didn't stop him looking guilty. That was the first time I felt really cross with him, disappointed too that he thought it was funny to scare an old woman half to death. But it didn't last long. I forgave him in a matter of seconds. After all, Gran had never liked him and she hadn't exactly welcomed him into the family from what Dad said. If he wanted to get his own back in a small way it was understandable. Even when Gran laid into *me* a few seconds later I couldn't really hold a grudge against him.

"It was you, wasn't it?" she accused, her eyes glassy with tears. "It's your silly idea of a joke, putting that man's photograph next to my bed."

"No," I protested but I could see that she didn't believe me. Neither did Mum.

"Well who was it then?" Gran said, spitting the words out. "It has to be you."

"Laura?" Mum was glaring at me.

I threw my hands up in despair. I mean Gran had a point. If I'd been in her position I'd probably have come to the same conclusion. The truth was just too unbelievable.

"That wasn't funny," I said to Dad later that day as we walked down to the village shop for a couple of lemons. Gran had to have a slice of lemon for her gin and tonic or the world would come to an end. "She could have had a heart attack."

"Not her," Dad said, "she's as strong as an ox. Anyway it was just a photo. I haven't actually metamorphosed right in front of her so that she can see me or anything like that."

I looked at him in horror. "I thought you said

that you weren't sure you could do that?"

He shrugged. "I'm not but I could give it a go. Even with people like your Gran, who don't believe in ghosts, it might work. It would be an interesting experiment."

"No!" I held up my hand. He stopped walking. "You mustn't do it. You've had your bit of fun but leave her alone now or you'll get us both into trouble."

He shrugged. "If you like."

But he looked a bit sulky and I felt bad that he'd only been here for a couple of days and already I was telling him off.

"Dad," I asked later as we took the long way through the fields back to the farm, "why *does* Gran dislike you so much?"

I threw the lemon into the air and ran forwards to catch it.

"No idea," Dad replied.

He shifted his eyes to the side momentarily and obviously caught sight of my dubious expression.

"I haven't. Cross my heart and hope to die. Well obviously I am dead – but you know what I mean."

I threw the lemon higher and higher. Some cows

looked up curiously.

"You must have some idea."

The lemon slipped straight through my fingers and fell to the ground. It landed with a splat right in the middle of a brand new steaming cowpat.

"Urgh! Now look what you've done," Dad said, almost seeming relieved at an opportunity to change the subject. "You can't pick that up. It's disgusting!"

We both stood staring at the gunk-splattered lemon. "It was the last one in the shop. I can't go back without it," I groaned.

"Just say there weren't any lemons left."

I shook my head. "She always seems to know if I'm lying. Besides, Mum will probably insist on driving all the way into town to get one for her and then she'll be ratty and..." I shrugged. "You get the picture."

I tried not to grimace at the thought of my fingers trying to lift up the lemon.

"It's just poo," I said.

"But you could contract some deadly disease," Dad said, stepping in front of me.

117

I gazed up at him. "You know what? This is one of those times when I could really do with a hug."

He held out his arms.

"Not a virtual hug, a proper hug, actual contact."

"I can't. I might hurt you. It's too risky."

"So is going back without this lemon," I murmured.

"What we really need is practical thinking here, Laura," Dad said.

"Well I could wrap some grass around it," I said, bending down to tear up the green stuff.

"No! Wait!" Dad said. "Before you do that I've got a better idea. I've got wind power."

I took a step back. "You're not going to fart, are you? The cow dung is bad enough without..."

He put his hands on his hips and tried to look shocked but I could tell he didn't mean it.

"No, Laura, I am not going to do such a thing. I am going to blow this lemon across the field like this."

He pursed his lips, puffed out his cheeks and a stream of air *bumpity bumped* the lemon along the grass in front of us. By time we reached the five-bar gate, a lot of the dung had been wiped off and I managed to wrap the lemon in a dock leaf so I wouldn't even touch it for the rest of the journey home. Dad and I did a sort of non-contact high five and congratulated ourselves on our teamwork when we reached the farm. It was weird but dropping that lemon had made me feel closer to him than ever.

"You haven't seen Liberty much," Mum said as we sat down to supper later that evening.

I watched and tried not to grimace as Gran drained the last of the gin and tonic, the lemon touching her lips.

Dad was there, propping his feet up on the end of the table, looking vaguely amused. Gran concentrated hard on her food, chewing slowly and thoroughly. She was unusually quiet.

"No," I replied. "I've texted a couple of times but she's been busy."

"I expect she'll find time in her hectic schedule to come around tomorrow morning," Gran muttered.

"Why's that?" Mum asked.

Gran made a strange sort of *harrumphing* sound and sawed into a sausage. "She just seems to have made a habit of dropping in on a Tuesday," she said.

"That's nice," Mum said.

"Where did you get these sausages from, Liz? They're not the ones I usually have, are they?"

Mum looked at me out of the corner of her eye. Dad swept his feet from the table, narrowly avoiding the salt cellar, and leaned forwards to do an imitation of Gran.

"They're not the ones I usually have, are they?" he mimicked.

I piled my fork with mashed potato and onion and concentrated hard to stop myself smiling. He could be so childish but at the same time he did make me laugh. Gran finished chewing and wiped her mouth.

"Do you know they're rather good," Gran said. "I think they're better than the sausages I usually buy. You can get those again, Liz."

I think Mum and I nearly fell off our chairs in surprise. Dad actually did. There was a *whoosh* and then a *thud* as he hit the floor.

"What on earth was that?" Mum gasped.

"Dunno," I said, desperately trying to cover for him, "maybe it was my feet banging against the

120

table leg."

"Oh, Laura," Mum said, "I do wish you wouldn't do that. Why can't you keep your legs still? You made me jump." She shivered. "I must be overtired. It suddenly feels very cold in here."

Gran was giving me one of her piercing gazes. I got up to clear the plates away and I didn't dare look at Dad, who was picking himself up and dusting himself down, because Gran was following my every move. It was as if she could see right inside my head.

Later that evening, I left Dad reading a book in my bedroom and sauntered into the kitchen to get a fresh glass of water to put by my bed. I was wearing a strappy nightdress which had shrunk slightly in the wash. I have to admit that it was pretty short.

"You'd better not flit around like that tomorrow morning," a voice resonated from the chair in the corner. Gran was sitting in the dark and I just about jumped out of my skin at the sound of her voice. Her skin was drained of colour as the moonlight flowed in through the window behind her.

"Gran, what are you doing?" I asked, my heart doing the quickstep inside my chest. "You scared me. I thought that you'd be in bed."

She was silent but still watching me.

"Can I put the light on?"

"If you like," she replied.

I flicked the switch on the Tiffany-style lamp that stood on the dresser and walked barefoot across the kitchen.

"Don't you have a dressing gown?" she asked.

"It's too hot for the summer, even in this house."

"Well Sam will be here at nine o'clock. He won't want to see you parading around in your nightwear."

Fine, I thought. I must remember to rummage in the attic during the night and hunt out some item of Victorian clothing that buttons up to the neck and sweeps down to the floor.

By some minor miracle I managed to keep the sarcasm to myself, sploshed some ice-cold water into my glass and took a gulp. The water tasted so fresh and clean up here – much nicer than in London.

"Who's Sam?"

"The gardener. I can't do it all on my own since

I did this." She slapped the side of her hip in disgust.

"I can help you if you like."

Whoa! I don't know where the words came from. I wasn't planning to say them. They just spurted out into the room before I could stop them. We both seemed equally stunned. In the half-light her eyes seemed to be glistening. I couldn't back out now.

"I could help you plant up the pots around the old well. I miss those colourful flowers."

There was a long pause. I wondered if she wasn't going to bother answering me or if she just didn't want my help.

"Thank you, Laura," she said, after what seemed like too long. "I'd like that."

She leaned heavily on the table as she tried to stand up. I put down my glass and went to help her.

"This stupid, stupid hip," she groaned and for once she didn't shrug me away.

Sam

The sound of the lawnmower woke me up the next morning, its throaty rumble chugging right beneath my window. "Do something about that, will you?" I groaned at Dad, pulling the pillow over my head.

There was no reply. I peeked out. He was nowhere to be seen. I turned over and tried to get back to sleep, tried not to worry about where he was, but it was no good. I had to go and find him. To make sure that he was still here.

"You've got serious trust issues, Laura," I said to myself as, remembering Gran's instructions from the previous night, I pulled on some shorts and a T-shirt. On my way downstairs I peered out of the long, rectangular landing window but there was no sign of the gardener and no sign of Dad either. The mower had stopped and there was such an unusual sound coming from the kitchen – it was Gran laughing. I couldn't remember the last time I'd heard her laugh. In fact, I couldn't remember ever hearing her laugh quite like that. I pushed open the kitchen door and there he was, the gardener, sitting at the table, sipping a mug of almost black coffee and eating one of the ginger flapjacks Dad had watched me make the day before.

"Ah, Laura!" Gran positively twinkled. "This is Sam, my gardener."

I must have looked completely gormless with my mouth hanging open and my eyes popping in disbelief. I'd expected someone old and crusty, all stooped and gnarled with weather-beaten skin and baggy trousers. Instead, there was the boy from the churchyard, his really long legs wrapped underneath the old oak chair, as if he didn't quite know what to do with them.

"Hi again!" He stood up and held out his hand.

"Hi," I whispered, acutely aware of the warmth of his palm against mine.

What sort of a teenager shook hands? I thought. Dad was right – he must be a bit strange.

Talking of which – where was Dad? My eyes darted all around the kitchen, even underneath the table and out of the windows, but either he had dematerialised or he really wasn't around. Briefly, I wondered where he had gone.

"Where's Mum?" I asked Gran, as Sam slid back onto his chair and took another piece of flapjack.

I moved to the range and put the kettle on the hot plate, hoping that if I stood there, Sam might think my puce face was due to the heat and not to shyness.

"She's gone to do a bit of shopping," Gran said. "I told her that I'd be fine while Sam's here to check I don't fall over or do anything silly."

She threw back her head and gave a girlish laugh. One of the tortoiseshell combs that she used in her upswept grey hair slipped slightly. I dragged my eyes away from Sam's leg where one brown knee was poking through a rip in his jeans.

"And me," I intercepted. "I can look after you too, you know."

She looked taken aback. "Yes, yes of course you can."

But I could tell she didn't mean it, didn't rate my

caring abilities. Sometimes I felt as if it wasn't just Dad who thought of me as four years old. It was as if I had a label stuck across my forehead – poor little Laura, the girl whose father was killed in an accident, the one whose life stopped when she was in reception at primary school.

"How are you settling in?" Sam asked, directing that clear blue gaze straight at me.

I felt so hot I wondered if I was about to spontaneously combust. I swear I saw Gran's ears prick up as she nibbled at one of her favourite shortbread biscuits and waited for my reply.

Get it right, Laura, I said to myself. Don't mess up with this. You can't tell the truth or she'll have it in for you even more and he'll think you're an absolute cow.

"It's fine."

No, no! Fine's not the right word. It's so non-committal. Say something else, say something more meaningful.

"I've been coming here on holiday for years. It's like my second home."

I swear Gran almost smiled at me, unless it

 127

was just a leftover from her gaze at Sam or maybe a touch of wind. I decided to allow myself a bit of brief congratulation anyway.

Better, Laura. Well done!

"Lucky you," he said.

Gran absolutely beamed then. I reckon if she could have got out of that chair without a struggle, she'd have leaped up and kissed him. Normally I'd have felt like putting my fingers down my throat and pretending to be sick but he really sounded as if he meant it. I sloshed some water into my mug and pressed down on the teabag.

"So, why haven't I seen you around before?" I asked.

"Oh Sam and his father only moved to the village just after Easter," Gran chirped up. "His father's our new vicar."

She was radiating approval now. Sam looked a bit embarrassed.

"Oh, *that's* why you were in the churchyard."

"Yeah!" He grinned. "I bet you thought I was a real nerd."

"No, of course not," I protested.

He raised one eyebrow.

"Well, maybe a bit," I confessed.

"I get paid a pittance to tidy around the gravestones," he explained, "and your gran's kindly given me some work as well. Now the holidays are here I can come earlier in the day instead of after school."

"That's nice," I said, aware that I sounded a complete and utter drip.

The back door creaked.

"Bang on cue," Gran muttered and a few seconds later the kitchen door was flung open. Liberty swanned in, all freshly washed hair and Optrexed eyes by the look of it.

"Granny!" she exclaimed, swooping towards her. "How *are* you today?"

She bent over and kissed Gran on the forehead.

"Much the same," Gran replied. "This is a nice surprise. You usually pop by in the afternoons."

"It's the holidays now, Granny, so I thought I'd come earlier."

"Fancy that!" Gran murmured. "And Sam's here early too."

Was Liberty the only person in the room who didn't pick up on the sarcasm?

"We were just on our way to the shop and Mum wondered if there was anything you wanted?"

"That's very kind, dear, but Laura nips down for me if I need anything."

"Oh!" Liberty said. "Of course. That's what I said to Mum but you know what she's like. She just wanted to double check."

She sent me a half smile before twirling around, her hair following in a glistening arc.

"Sam," she virtually chirruped, "I'd completely forgotten you'd be here today."

Yeah right, I thought, and accidentally dropped my spoon into the sink from quite a height. The clatter didn't put her off at all.

"How are you?" she cooed.

"Good, thanks."

Was it my imagination or did he look a bit uncomfortable? Were his hands clutching his mug a little more tightly, his feet crossed over one another in an unnatural pose, toes pressing down against the flagstone floor? He fancies her, I thought, but he doesn't want to admit it, at least not in front of Gran and me.

"I haven't seen you around much," she said, throwing him a coy smile.

"No, I've been busy."

"Oh me too," Liberty replied.

I leaned back against the metal rail of the range and blew the steam away from my tea. It was like being at the theatre and watching a scene playing out. Sam stared into his mug. There was one of those awkward silences that make the air feel as if it's made of thin, brittle glass.

"Actually I wanted to speak to Laura," Liberty said at last, her face falling, "to say I'm sorry I haven't been in touch. And about the other day – I was in a bit of a mood. Sorry."

Nobody looked at me but I knew that they were waiting for my reply. She obviously hadn't really come around to see me so it took a while to summon up an element of grace from the depths of my soul.

"It's okay," I mumbled. "It was probably my fault."

"No. It was mine. All mine. Everything's been so stressful for us but it's not been easy for you either, moving up here. I should have been more understanding. I should have put all of *my* problems to one side."

Her voice was weaving us all into its compassionate web. She came over and hugged me while I wondered how pressing her problems really were. I could smell the grassy notes of her new perfume and the fruity scent of her shampoo. She was just so glossy and glamorous and I felt like a tramp beside her. I also had this feeling, deep down, that she was putting on a bit of an act, but Gran was beaming, so she seemed convinced of Liberty's sincerity.

"So, Sam," Liberty turned away but linked her arm through mine, "have you got plans for the summer? Are you going away?"

"No," he said. "Dad can't afford the time off, as we've just moved here."

"Oh that's a shame," Liberty sympathised, "but never mind, you can always give me a call if you're stuck for things to do."

He smiled and I thought that I detected the

slightest hint of colour rising behind his freckles.

"Thanks, Liberty. I'll remember that." He turned to look at me. "And there's Laura too, of course."

I started with surprise that he should include me. Liberty tensed. Imperceptible if we hadn't been in bodily contact but it was definitely there.

"Yes, of course," she said, "we mustn't leave Laura out, must we?"

Sam scraped back his chair. "I'd better be getting on," he said to Gran. "Thanks for the coffee."

"Oh don't rush off because of me," Liberty protested.

He smiled and turned, looking her square in the face. "I'm not. I've got work to do." He headed for the door. "Great flapjack by the way, Laura."

"Thanks," I said, any pleasure at his praise evaporating as a result of the way Liberty yanked her arm away from mine.

Protection

"Have you been all right?"

Dad rushed across the garden while Mum was still emptying shopping bags from the car. I was lying on a rug reading a book.

"Yes," I hissed. "Of course I have. Where have you been?"

He flopped down beside me. "I thought I'd take a trip into town with your mother, just for old times' sake." He looked at my watch. "We've been so much longer than I thought. Her driving hasn't got any better."

"I don't know what you mean. Mum's a good driver, most of the time."

"Just so slow," Dad groaned, "and I kept thinking of you here, all on your own."

I laughed and Mum looked over towards me.

"Something funny in the book," I called back.

"Do you want a hand with those bags?"

She shook her head. "This is the last one."

"I wasn't on my own," I whispered to Dad, "Gran was here."

"Well she wouldn't be any good if anything happened."

"Dad, I'm not still a baby. What could happen?"

"All sorts of things. Your world is full of danger."

I reached out a hand. "You mustn't worry so much. Uncle Pete's probably within shouting distance somewhere on the farm. Besides, Sam was here and Liberty popped around for a while so I haven't been lonely."

He straightened up. "Who's Sam?"

"Gran's gardener."

He relaxed again and lay back down. It was weird because I could almost see the red checked pattern of the rug through his body.

"He's the boy we saw at the churchyard."

That was a mistake. He was sitting up again in no time at all.

"I knew that he was going to be trouble the minute I set eyes on him."

 135

"He's not trouble. He's nice."

"How old is he?"

"I don't know. I didn't ask."

Dad raked his hands through his hair. "Did he ask you out?"

"No, of course not. He's not going to be interested in me when Liberty's around, is he?"

"Why on earth do you say that? Of course he is," Dad insisted.

I smiled at him. "Thanks, but I know I'm not in her league in the looks department."

"Yes, you are," Dad said vehemently. "You're beautiful."

"You *are* a bit biased."

He looked at me and sighed. "My beautiful Laura – that's what I used to call you."

"I don't remember that."

"No, I don't suppose you do." He frowned. "Anyway, boys aren't totally fixated on how pretty a girl is. It's not just about looks."

"Isn't it? You could have fooled me."

He leaned back on his elbows. "Hasn't your mother taught you anything? Boys like girls with a bit of character, a sense of humour, kindness shining out of them – girls just like you, Laura."

I blushed. "I think you're a bit out of date there, Dad. Maybe back in the dark ages but—"

He sat bolt upright, making me jump.

"I forbid you to see him."

"Don't be silly. You can't do that. We're not in the Victorian era. Besides, I'm bound to see him around the village."

I peered up at him.

"You're jealous."

"I am not. I am just a concerned and responsible father."

"Well there's no need to be – concerned, I mean. Liberty's obviously claimed him already. Her tongue was virtually hanging out."

"Laura, that's a horrible expression!"

"Well it's true. You're easily shocked, aren't you?"

He frowned. "I just want what's best for my favourite daughter."

"You've only got one daughter, haven't you?" I teased. "So I've got to be your favourite, haven't I?"

He was very still suddenly and had a slightly strange look on his face. It was only for a second or two, one of those instances that stirs up a slight sense of unease but it's so fractional, and the feeling is so deep, that you bury it almost straight away. Besides, Dad blew me a kiss and summoned up one of his broad smiles.

"Of, course you're my favourite girl, Laura. Never, ever doubt it."

So I didn't. I never had.

TRUST

A couple of days later Gran asked me if I'd put some flowers on Grandad's grave. She sat in her chair in the kitchen and barked instructions through the window while I cut velvety pink roses, big white daisies and large sprigs of rosemary.

"I thought this was just for cooking," I said.

"Rosemary is for remembrance too," Gran replied.

I tucked it in amongst the roses.

"That's nice," I said. "I shall think of that every time Mum puts it with some roast lamb."

"Your grandad liked roast lamb," Gran said. "I could make my own mint jelly to go with it back in the day. Not now though."

She shifted awkwardly in the chair and winced.

I went inside, put the flowers on the table and adjusted the cushion behind her back.

"You'll make mint jelly again soon, Gran," I said.

"You're a good girl, Laura. Your grandad always said that you had a nice nature."

The words startled me. Not that Grandad had thought them but that Gran had told me.

"Oh! Did he?" I felt a warmth blossom behind my ribcage. "I used to love spending time with him."

"I know you did, pet."

I bit my lip, picked up the flowers and left the room before she could see the sudden tears shimmying down my cheeks. Never in my whole fourteen years did I remember her calling me 'pet' before.

Dad was by the front gate, kicking a small stone.

"Where are you going with those flowers?" he asked.

"To the churchyard. To put them on Grandad's grave." I wiped my eyes on my sleeve.

"Are you all right?" He fell into step beside me. "Have you been crying?"

"Not really. I'm just being silly."

"What you need is company," Dad said.

Actually what I really wanted at that particular moment was to be on my own but I couldn't tell him that. He wouldn't have understood. We walked in silence so he obviously had picked up a bit on my mood.

I thought about Grandad and how much I missed him. One of my earliest memories was clutching his work-roughened hand as he led me out to the orchard to feed the chickens. I was probably only about two and a half but I can still remember his strength and the way he clasped me to him, as if I was the most precious thing in his whole world.

First of all we would go to the old dairy where the grain was kept in a big metal drum. Grandad would lift me onto a wooden stool so that I could reach and then, holding me firmly around the middle, he would flip open the lid and pass me a little metal bowl to plunge into the silky grain. The corn was like a cascade of golden pearls running over my chubby babyish fingers. I loved that feeling. Sometimes I would plunge my hand straight into the barrel, grabbing a handful of the cool grain and listening to the plinking sound it made as it fell like hailstones into mine or

Grandad's bowl.

The chickens always came running and squawking towards us the second they heard Grandad lift the latch on the orchard gate. We would toss the corn high into the air and laugh as the hens pecked at the ground as if they hadn't eaten for weeks.

While they were feeding we would collect the eggs. I had a special little basket, woven from willow and lined with flowery fabric by Aunt Jane. Liberty had one too. When we got older, Liberty and I were allowed to go on our own to collect the eggs. She knew of all the secret places where the hens laid. Speckle, the little grey bantam, liked to play hide and seek with her eggs. Underneath the raised shed where Gran kept her bike was one of her favourite places. Speckle had scratched out a deep hollow in the dry, dusty ground and we had to stretch our arms as far as they would go so that we could reach those eggs.

If one of the hens got broody and wouldn't move, you had to scoop your hand right underneath them. I was always a bit afraid of getting pecked but Liberty was fearless. She'd laugh at my nervousness and then drop the warm egg, maybe with a downy feather or two attached, into my outstretched palm. I loved the smoothness of the pale brown shells, the way the egg nestled in my cupped hand and the feeling of gentle heat against my skin.

Life seemed less complicated then. I still loved feeding the chickens and watching them excavate their funny bunker-type holes in the grass so that they could have a dust bath. But sometimes I felt a bit sorry for them, especially when they flew up into the apple trees, perching uneasily on the lower, gnarled branches. They couldn't get any higher than that. I wondered if they looked up at the other birds soaring high in the sky and felt envious. If I'm honest, I felt envious of Liberty because she could have had all the time in the world with Grandad, if she'd wanted to.

"Did you and Grandad get on okay?" I asked Dad as I removed the dead flowers from the front of the headstone and replaced them with the fresh ones.

Dad was pacing up and down. "Your grandad got on with everyone," he said.

"All the same," I persisted, walking to the

corner of the church where there was an outside tap, "considering Gran really, really didn't like you…"

"Your grandad always saw the best in people."

"Well I don't suppose there was any 'worst' to see, was there?" I joked.

"We've all got a dark side, Laura. We've all done things we're not proud of." Suddenly he sounded deadly serious.

I let the tap run, the icy water gushing all over my bare toes. I winced.

"What do you mean?"

I looked at him. He didn't look back. Instead he kept his head down and feet moving, studying the tarmac path.

"I mean that people aren't always who you think they are."

He was talking in riddles and I didn't like it.

"What are you trying to say?"

There was a silence, both of us standing there with this great chasm between us. He looked up, straight into my eyes, and opened his mouth but then he stopped, something over my shoulder distracting him.

"Dad?"

144

"Nothing. I'm not saying anything. Can we go, Laura? I'm not very keen on graveyards. They spook me out."

"In a minute," I replied, turning off the tap. "I've got to give the flowers some water. I bet you wouldn't be so impatient if it was me or Penny tending to *your* grave."

"Who?"

I headed back over the grass, lugging the watering can. He was close on my heels now.

"Penny, your cousin, duh? The other person who used to put flowers on your grave. Didn't you know that she did that?"

I knelt down, made a gap in Grandad's flowers and filled up the reservoir with water.

"No, yes. I mean, I forgot because your flowers are so much nicer."

I beamed. When he praised me I just felt happiness bubbling up inside.

"Her flowers *were* pretty. I wanted to get in touch and say thank you but Mum said that Penny has moved house and she's lost her new number. I don't suppose you could find out where she lives, could you?"

Dad suddenly looked slightly alarmed. "No, I don't think I could do that."

I frowned. "I suppose it would mean you wafting down to London to try to track her down and it could take ages and…" I smiled up at him, "… I'd rather keep you here with me. I don't want you getting lost."

He smiled back and looked relieved. Then he frowned again.

"Uh oh!" he groaned. "Here comes trouble."

When I stood up and turned around Sam was loping towards me. Dad may not have been pleased to see him but I was. My heart definitely started to beat a little faster.

"Hi!" I called. "Fancy seeing you here!"

"Yeah!" he said with a grin. "It's not exactly a conventional place to hang out, is it? Nice flowers, by the way."

"Thanks. They're from Gran's garden."

"I know."

Stupid of me. Of course he did. We stood facing each other, locked in one of those shy, clunky pauses. Out of the corner of my eye I could see Dad beckoning towards the road.

"I'd better be getting back," I said to Sam.

"Do you have to?"

"Well no, I don't suppose so, not straight away."

Dad slapped his hand to his forehead and sighed. A little windmill on one of the graves began to spin.

"Do you want to come back to mine for a glass of lemonade or a cup of tea? We've got cupboards full of tea. I think it's in the job description – become vicar, provide plenty of tea."

I smiled and turned away from Dad who by now was gesticulating wildly, shaking his head, drawing his hand across his throat in a totally over the top way. The windmill spun faster and faster. I thought Sam might say something but he didn't take his eyes from my face.

"I've even got my own personal entrance and exit to the churchyard," Sam said, pointing to a rickety wooden gate tucked into a corner of the hawthorn hedge.

"Well, what girl could refuse that invitation?" I joked.

"Give me a minute and I'll put that watering can back for you."

He reached out and brushed my fingers with his. I bit my lip, watched as he jogged over to the standpipe and stopped to talk to an elderly lady.

"I'll get rid of him," Dad said, turning to head off in Sam's direction.

"No, you won't!"

I tried to get hold of him but my hand wafted straight through his arm. He stopped though. Looked down. He'd obviously felt something. I didn't feel anything, just a crescent of cool air. "I don't like him hanging around you all the time."

I half laughed. "He's not hanging around me. This is only the third time I've seen him. I thought you'd want me to make friends. I mean, you were an only child too. You know what it's like." I sighed into the warm summer day. "It's just a glass of lemonade, Dad, or a cup of tea. You know, that stuff that grows on bushes in India. I think it comes from the camellia family and by the time it gets over here it's in a packet and you add hot water and—"

"I don't want you to be on your own, especially

not with him."

"I've noticed that," I replied drily.

"I'll come with you."

"No, Dad, it's fine. I don't need a chaperone."

"You can't be too careful. This vicar's son thing is a great cover. He's too good to be true."

I twisted my lips into what must have been a particularly unattractive expression. He just wouldn't take a hint.

"Dad, I'd really rather you didn't."

He looked extremely put out, shocked even.

"But, Laura, what if… he, you know, tries it on?"

I tried not to laugh. "I think it's unlikely."

Worse luck, I thought, and hoped that Dad couldn't read my mind. I tugged at my hair.

"Look, my hair needs washing. I'm wearing my oldest shorts and well… I'm sure he doesn't see me like that. He just wants to be friends, that's all."

"The trouble with you, Laura, is that you're too trusting."

"And the trouble with you, Dad, is that you're not trusting enough."

The words were out before I had the chance to

stop them. His face fell. He looked as if I'd slapped him.

"I'm sorry. I didn't mean that." Actually, yes I did. "Look, I won't be long. If I get into trouble I'll call you. You'll hear me, won't you?"

"Maybe I will. Maybe I won't," he replied.

"Don't be like that. Please. It's nice to know that you're there, protecting me."

I wanted to tell him to stop being so childish but I managed to hold those words back. They wouldn't have helped. Sam was making his way towards me. Surreptitiously I blew Dad a little kiss. His sulkiness softened.

"I'll be fine. Don't worry. I'll see you later, back at home?"

He nodded. "If you're sure?"

"I am."

But as I walked over to join Sam I couldn't help but let Dad's words get to me. I hardly knew anything about this boy. Maybe Sam *was* too good to be true. Maybe Dad was right and I *was* too trusting.

SHARING

The house was modern but built from local stone, with a slate roof.

"The original rectory is over the other side of the wall," he said, pointing to a big house with tall, elegant windows. "I suppose it just got too expensive to run so the Church sold it off and built this instead."

He pushed open the holly-green door and ushered me inside his house.

There was a little lobby, where a pile of shoes had taken up residence, and two doors to either side. The one on the right led straight into the kitchen. Sam said the one on the left was his dad's study and I could hear the tapping of computer keys.

"So, what would you like – tea or homemade lemonade?"

"Lemonade, please."

I watched as he took two tall glasses from a cupboard and opened the fridge.

"Ice?"

I nodded and suddenly wished that I hadn't come. And why oh why had I put on this tatty coral-coloured T-shirt and my old blue-and-white striped shorts? I could have been wearing my favourite summer dress with the deep pink roses on it and lacing up the back or the new turquoise jeans with my favourite strappy top. Anything that would have made me feel a bit less grungy and more confident.

"Shall we go outside?" he suggested.

I followed him across the lawn towards a wooden table and four chairs set up under a weeping willow tree. There was a tabby cat stretched out on the sunny side of the table. She lifted her head and *miaow*ed at Sam. "Say hello to Cleo," Sam said, scratching behind her ears.

"Hello, Cleo," I said, touching her soft, stripy fur. "Nice to meet you."

"She likes you," Sam said, as the cat began to purr. "She doesn't take to everyone."

I sat down, feeling pleased with myself, as if I had passed some sort of test.

Cleo slithered off the table and onto my lap. I could feel the tips of her claws against my leg but it didn't matter. I felt really honoured.

"I've always wanted a cat but Mum's never been keen," I said. "She thinks they're a tie. I think it's because she grew up on a farm. When she was little they could hardly ever go away on holiday because of the animals." I took a sip of my lemonade. "This is delicious. Did your mum make it?"

You know when you've said the wrong thing, how there's this shift in the air around you, as if someone is tapping you on the shoulder saying, "Oops, you shouldn't have said that"?

Momentarily, Sam stared down at the bobbing ice cubes in his glass and I bit my lip, prepared to say sorry for whatever can of worms I'd just opened.

"My mum died. Last year."

"Oh, I'm sorry. I didn't know."

"That's why we moved here. Dad wanted a fresh start. We'd been at the last parish since I was a baby. Everyone rallied around but…" He tailed off, fished a small thunderfly out of his drink. "They all meant well but it got a bit claustrophobic, and then there were the women who saw an opportunity to install themselves permanently in the vicarage."

"Really? That quickly?"

I couldn't hide my shock.

"Yeah. Haven't you had a similar thing with your mum?"

"No!"

"You're lucky. Within a couple of months of Mum dying, they were like bees to a honeypot or whatever the expression is, knocking on the door with endless pies and cakes and big doe eyes."

"That's awful!"

He shrugged. "That's what people are like."

"They don't sound like your ideal congregation."

He leaned back in his chair and shielded his eyes from the sun. I wasn't sure whether to change the subject or not but my curiosity got the better of me.

"Was it sudden, your mum?"

"No, she was ill for ages. Breast cancer. We thought she'd beaten it a couple of times."

"You got time to say goodbye though?" I hated myself the minute I said it. How could I be so callous? "Not that that makes it any easier. I didn't mean…"

He smiled. "I know what you mean, Laura. And yes, we got plenty of time to say goodbye." The willow leaves swished in the breeze. "Not like you."

His words were almost lost, almost carried away and up into the sky.

"Your gran told me about your dad's accident. She says it's been really tough for you and your mum."

My eyes widened then. I coughed slightly as the tartness of a small piece of lemon stung the back of my throat.

"Did she say that?"

He frowned slightly. "Of course. You can't hide much from your gran. She doesn't miss a thing."

"It's just that we've never really got on. I've always thought that she didn't like me. She didn't like Dad, you see, and I think that I remind her of him. Have you got grandparents?"

155

"Yes, both sets. I'm lucky. And I've got a sister too but she's not here at the moment. She's on a gap year, travelling around Australia."

He shifted on his chair and took something out of his back pocket. He leaned towards me, holding out his hand.

"That's my mum."

I took the photograph and looked at a laughing, kind-eyed woman with a smattering of freckles and sandy-coloured hair, just like Sam's.

"She's lovely."

He nodded and I handed the photo back. He stared at it.

"I miss her loads. Does it get any better, Laura? Does it get any easier?"

I was taken aback, didn't know what to say. I paused, tried to conjure up a whole list of comforting words. But in the end I just had to be honest.

"I think that when you've lost someone really close, like a parent or brother or sister, you live your life slightly differently to other people."

I was quiet for a moment. So was he.

"On the outside you look the same as everyone

else, except some people can't hide the sadness behind their eyes. It's not a sadness that makes you miserable all the time. It's more a sense of incompleteness, a feeling that on the inside you're different because you can never be sure of anything ever again. Because whatever, whoever you love might be taken away in an instant."

I stopped talking for a moment. He was listening so intently, as if his life depended upon it, as if everything *I* had felt was going to be true for him too. I was going to stop there, because that can't be the case, can it? Everyone's different. Everyone must feel different things and handle death in different ways. That's why I don't usually tell people how I feel. To be honest, mostly they don't ask and I get the feeling that the ones who do take an interest in long-term grief would prefer the airbrushed version. But Sam's silence and the willow tree, which rustled encouragement, compelled me to carry on.

"It does get better but there's always the feeling that there's something missing, like a bit of your heart has been chipped away. And there are some days, the days when something special is happening or everything is going wrong, when you feel completely alone and…"

I bit my lip, felt the tears well up, concentrated hard on stroking the top of Cleo's head.

"… on those days, no, it doesn't feel any better. I'm sorry. That's not what you wanted to hear."

He reached out and brushed my hand, just for a second. "No, you're wrong. That's just what I wanted to hear because I could tell it was the truth."

I swallowed, sniffed, prayed my eyes wouldn't well over. "It was *my* truth. It doesn't mean that it will be like that for you."

"I know that," he said, "but it still helps. Even though it happened ages ago, you must still miss your dad a lot."

What could I say to that? Actually, no, because he's around and, irritatingly, I've just spotted the wishy-washy top of his head as he paces up and down behind the hawthorn hedge. I forced my thoughts backwards a couple of weeks to the time before Dad came back to me.

"Most people think that because I was so young

when it happened I don't remember what it was like to have Dad around. It's that silly phrase 'you don't miss what you've never had'. But I do remember Dad being around and even though my memories might be fuzzy, I still miss him. I still get that sharp, slicing pain like a massive paper cut when I want to tell him something or need his advice. Just because he went away a long time ago doesn't mean I don't still need him. People don't seem to get that."

Sam nodded as if he understood. "I don't know whether Dad was right to move us away," he said. "Part of me wanted to stay in that house where Mum lived. Did you feel that? Has it made you feel further away from your dad, moving to Derbyshire?" Another impossible question.

"My mum says that Dad will follow us wherever we go."

"And you believe that?"

This was one question I could answer with certainty.

"Yes," I said firmly. "I really do."

Jealousy

"What were you talking about?" Dad fell into step beside me as I walked home.

"Things."

"What sort of things?"

"You probably know exactly what we were saying because you were skulking around listening to us."

He put his hand to his heart area.

"Laura, how could you think I could do such a thing? I respect your privacy."

"Yeah right! I saw you in the churchyard."

"That's only because I was worried about you. I wanted to make sure you were safe."

He certainly knew how to make me feel guilty.

"I'm sorry. I know. But hey look," I threw back my head and stretched out my arms, "I'm okay. I survived drinking a glass of lemonade with a boy!"

I smiled at him. I couldn't be cross for long.

The conversation with Sam had taken me back to how I used to feel and now that Dad was here I could pack all of those insecurities up and dump them in the dustbin. I could move on, grow in confidence with Dad by my side. Always.

Aunt Jane was just leaving when I got back to the farm. I waved as she backed the car out of the driveway but she didn't respond, just revved the engine hard and sped off down the road.

Mum was in the kitchen, her face crumpling as she fought against tears.

"What's the matter?"

I looked around. Gran wasn't sitting in her favourite chair, waiting for lunch.

"Is it Gran? Has something happened?"

I was surprised at how worried I felt. Mum sniffed and grabbed a tissue from the box on the dresser.

"No, your gran's fine. She's in the sitting room watching *Bargain Hunt*."

Relief.

"What then? Is it Aunt Jane?"

Dad was standing very close to Mum. I could

 161

tell he wanted to put his arms around her.

"I don't understand her," Mum said. "I thought she'd be glad we'd moved up here, that I was taking the pressure off her. I thought that's what she wanted."

"It was. So what's her problem?"

"I don't know," Mum groaned. "She just seems to criticise everything I do. She's worse than your grandmother." Mum managed a weak smile. "And that's saying something."

"Liberty's been a bit weird too. I thought I'd see more of her."

Mum came and wrapped her arms around me while Dad whisked a circle around the three of us with his finger. It looked like the faintest of jet trails whispering through the air. Mum didn't seem to see or notice anything different but, for a few moments, I felt so safe, safer than I'd ever felt before – just the three of us standing there together. It was good. I wanted to be able to remember that feeling for ever, to be able to reach out and reel it in whenever I was feeling stressed or sad.

"I suppose it's a big change for everyone," Mum said, her voice muffled against my hair. "Perhaps it's just taking time for things to settle down."

I squeezed her a little tighter.

"Yeah, I'm sure you're right," I said. "She's just gone a bit overboard with the older sister thing. She'll get over it."

Mum lifted her head, pushed me away slightly.

"You think?" she asked with a wry smile.

"Well," I replied, "maybe not totally."

Maybe it was better I hadn't got any brothers and sisters. Sometimes they could cause a lot of grief.

"What shall we do this afternoon?" Dad asked after lunch.

"I'm going to help Gran plant some geraniums," I replied. "Mum's bought a load from the garden centre. We're going to put them on the old well. I thought it might make her feel better."

Dad tried not to wrinkle up his nose in disapproval but didn't totally succeed.

"That's nice," he said. "But what am I going to do?"

He sounded like a small child.

"Well, you could watch us, but that might be

 163

a bit boring. Mum's off into town again to pick up Gran's prescription. You could go with her. She may not be able to see you but I bet it's still nice to spend time together, isn't it?"

He seemed to like that idea and to be honest I felt quite relieved. I was beginning to feel like an insect under a microscope with Dad hovering over me all of the time. Once I'd done my good deed of the day with Gran I hoped to snatch a bit of time to myself.

Gran sat in a tall upright wicker chair and in front of her Mum and I positioned an old garden table spread with newspaper. We rang Uncle Pete on his mobile and asked him to come and lift the bag of compost out of the shed but he was at the far end of the fields so in the end Mum and I managed it ourselves. There were nine red geraniums, some pots of little white daisies, three trailing fuchsias, some silvery plants, which Gran couldn't remember the name of, and trays of alyssum and lobelia. I set all the plants out on the grass in front of Gran and put three large terracotta pots on the table.

"Let's put some of those broken bits of pot in the bottom, Laura," Gran instructed. "That helps with the drainage. So the plants don't get all waterlogged."

I did as I was told and then filled the pots two thirds full with compost. Next I passed the first geranium over to Gran. She lifted the plant to her nose and smelled the leaves.

"Oh, Laura," she said, almost shivering with delight. "This is wonderful. I feel as if I'm coming back to life again."

She plunged her hands into the prepared pots and positioned the geranium in place. We worked together for about an hour, occasionally chatting, but mostly asking each other where to put a particular plant. She didn't criticise me once. In fact, just the opposite.

"That looks lovely, Laura," she said when I placed the last bit of lobelia in the final pot. "You've made a really good job of that."

I blushed. I wasn't used to being praised by her but it was actually quite a nice feeling.

Later I made us a cup of tea and took it out into the garden. "Gran," I asked, as I sank onto a rug next to her chair, "do you know what's wrong with Aunt Jane? She's upsetting Mum. Also,

Liberty's not been around as much as I'd hoped. I thought we'd spend loads of time together."

Gran placed her teacup carefully into the saucer and sighed. "They're like peas in a pod, those two," she said, stroking her chin. "Actually, I think I probably do know what the problem is. They're jealous."

"Of who?" I asked.

"Well, Liberty's jealous of you, and Jane has always been jealous of your mother, ever since they were little girls."

She paused, stirred her tea for the second time.

"But that's ridiculous," I said, trying to take in this unbelievable information.

"Maybe, but it's true. I expect Pete and Jane are worried they won't do so well out of my will now that you're here to look after me. They've got their eye on this house too. Jane's been itching to get me out of here for years so that she can move in."

"Oh, Gran, I'm sure that's not true. I know she says they could do with more space but—"

"But I won't be here for ever," Gran interrupted.

"That's not what I was going to say." I bit my lip. "I was going to say that *we* won't be here for too long."

It sounded horrible as I said it. As if I couldn't wait to get away.

"What I mean is that when you're better Mum and I will probably get a house of our own."

Gran's eyes flashed behind her sparse grey lashes. "And then your aunt will be on at me to move to somewhere smaller. But she'll have to wait. I started my married life in this house, Laura. This is where I raised my family. This is where your grandfather and I spent nearly fifty years together. Every room here is full of memories. I'm not ready to move out yet and *no one* is going to push me. At least she can't say your mother is shirking her responsibilities any more."

I looked up at her, wide-eyed.

"Oh yes, Laura. I knew what Jane was implying or probably even saying. I may be old and decrepit but I don't miss much."

"They had this big row," I said. "It was not long after your fall. Aunt Jane and Uncle Pete were really horrible to Mum and I suppose Liberty's been a bit different since then. I tried to understand that she was just siding with Aunt Jane but I thought that once we moved up here we'd all pull together like a proper family does."

"Ah," Gran said, with a curt laugh, "a proper family. One where everyone is content and no one resents anyone else."

I nodded.

Gran dropped her hand onto the top of my head. It was warm and heavy. Comforting.

"I'm afraid, Laura, that 'proper families' only really exist in books. Real life is a lot messier than that."

We both fell silent but she left her hand where it was and I didn't move, didn't want to disturb it. I thought about Liberty and what Gran had said about her. I thought back to Christmas, the last time she'd come to London. "You don't know how lucky you are," she'd said. "Your mum's got plenty of time for you. My mum spends all of her time working or cooking or acting as a referee between the boys."

"My mum works too," I said, "and even if you've got loads of friends, being an only child can be a bit lonely sometimes."

"Nah!" she'd disagreed, as if she knew exactly

what it was like to be me. "It's got to be better than having annoying brothers."

"You don't mean that," I said.

She pulled a face. "You've seen how they start something and I get the blame. It's not fair."

I twisted my lips in a show of sympathy.

"And if we go out for the day we have this silly voting system and the boys always end up winning – unless you're there."

"You don't do too badly, Liberty," I said.

"But you do better," she flashed back, leaping up and flinging open my wardrobe doors.

She yanked a new top from one of the hangers. The label was still attached. I'd been waiting for just the right opportunity to wear it. "Can I borrow this?"

I didn't even hesitate. "Of course. It'll probably suit you better than me anyway."

She tried it on. I was right. The sapphire blue was the perfect backdrop for her long blond hair and the silky fabric clung to her curves in all the right places. I was still waiting for my curves to appear but I had the horrible feeling that I was going to remain 'willowy', as Mum put it. To me that was a nice way of saying that I'd probably end up with a body like a boy.

"You're too nice, Laura," Liberty had said, twirling in front of the mirror and then coming over to give me a hug.

Yeah, I thought to myself as she crushed the blue top between us. You're right, Lib. Sometimes I am.

Revelations

It didn't take much to tire Gran so, after we'd finished our tea, I helped her back to bed.

"I never used to have a rest in the afternoon," she complained. "I was always busy doing things."

"I know," I said, helping her to lift her legs up and onto the bed.

"Probably *too* busy," she murmured. "I should have stopped all that cooking and cleaning and gardening and spent a bit more time with you when you came to stay."

I stopped, still holding onto her ankles.

"It's okay."

She shook her head. "No, it's not. I was stupid, holding on to grievances for so long. Taking them out on you. None of what happened is your fault."

She closed her eyes. I covered her with the rose-pink throw from the bottom of the bed.

"It's no fun getting old, Laura."

I hated it when people said that. Some people would leap at the chance to get old. Dad for one.

"It's better than the alternative though, isn't it?" I replied, not meaning to sound sharp.

Her eyelids fluttered open. She looked straight at me, as if she could see all of those tumultuous thoughts churning around inside my head.

"Yes, I suppose it is. That was thoughtless of me."

I shrugged. "It's okay. I was being a bit touchy."

"I think you're entitled to be. After all, thanks to me, your life's been turned upside down, hasn't it? I'm sorry, Laura. For everything."

"You didn't fall off that ladder on purpose," I murmured.

On impulse I took a couple of steps, bent down and kissed her on the forehead.

Her eyes suddenly looked glassy. The last thing I wanted was for her to cry. Didn't know what I'd do. So I turned away quickly to draw the curtains, to hide my confusion. I'd never seen this side of Gran before and just didn't know how to respond.

The library van had been to the village a couple

of days earlier and I'd chosen a pile of books to read. I lay on the sofa, cushions squashed behind my head, pool of sunlight warming my arms, but I couldn't concentrate. All I could think about was what Gran had said about Liberty's jealousy. I didn't want to believe it. People who loved each other weren't jealous, were they? Besides, Liberty was the one with the looks, the figure, the brains. There was absolutely no reason for her to be jealous of me, but if it wasn't that, what was it? There was definitely something that was causing her to be a bit distant and I wanted to sort it out. I wanted to prove that Gran was wrong and that I knew Lib better than she did. So as soon as Mum got back I headed off to the end of the village.

"Laura," Dad said, running and flapping his arms as if they were wings, in order to keep up with me, "where are you going in such a tearing hurry?"

"To see Lib," I huffed. "To clear the air."

"Oh! Does it need clearing?"

"Yes, of course it does. She's my best friend in the whole world and something's wrong between us. I don't know what it is but I want to find out."

Dad looked anxious. "Maybe you ought to think about this first," he said, floating in front of me. "You might say something that you regret. You might find out something that you don't want to know."

I stopped. "Like what?"

He wouldn't meet my eyes.

"Do you know something?"

"No, of course not. I just don't want you to be hurt."

"Well I'm hurt already because she's not coming round or making time for me and she's taking ages to reply to my texts. All of those things are making me hurt." I swerved around him. "It'll be fine. Liberty and I are as close as sisters. We can say anything to each other. We'll be able to thrash it out, whatever *it* is."

"Oh dear," Dad groaned, "that sounds violent."

"It's a figure of speech," I said. "I didn't mean it literally."

"Oh thank goodness for that," he said. "I do so hate it when fights break out."

But things did get physical and by trying to make everything better I just ended up making it worse.

I know a lot about jealousy now. It's like vinegar.

It eats away at you, sharpens you around the edges until you are brittle and hard. But it can hide itself underneath a veneer of familiarity. In the end though, the cracks appear, however much you think that you love each other. Jealousy shrivels your heart until it is like one of those dried up mushrooms that Mum puts in risotto. Porcini they're called.

Jealousy has such tenacity. It hangs on by its fingertips waiting for its moment. I'd never noticed it in Liberty's face before, never felt it in her hug, heard it curling out of her lips in snakelike words. She could be sharp, of course. She got that from Gran. But I'd never detected the years of suppressed resentment until that day when I tried to put things right.

It had been going quite well. Liberty even seemed pleased to see me. She was lying in the hammock strung between two apple trees when I got to her house. She lifted her head, swung her feet out into a sitting position and gave me a brief hug. Things were looking up until she mentioned some friend of hers whose dad was talking about test-driving a Ferrari. She began to moan about Uncle Pete and his fifteen-year-old estate car and then she started on her lifestyle and all of the things she couldn't have. So that's when I made the mistake.

"Life's not about how much money you've got, Liberty."

"Easy for you to say."

The words shot out faster than if she'd been using Luke's catapult. I should have backed away then but I didn't. I just allowed myself to be all hot-headed and defensive.

"I don't know what you mean. Mum's worked hard for everything we have. She's never had any help from anyone. You're the one in the family who gets Gran to buy you presents or give you extra pocket money."

Liberty's eyes glittered dangerously behind an extravagant application of purple mascara. "Well my dad says that if Gran goes gaga, you and your mum could get your hands on everything now you're living there."

I gasped. "Don't be stupid. We don't want Gran's money. That's not why we're here. Anyway you're talking as if she's completely senile and she's not."

The "Huh," that emerged from her mouth was like projectile vomit splattering me with rancid disbelief. I felt so stupid, standing there looking into her face full of fury. For years I'd wanted to be just like her, to have her cool blond looks and crisp self-esteem. I'd thought that I knew her as well as I knew myself. "You think they had the perfect marriage, don't you?"

"What are you talking about now?"

"Your parents. You think they were so happy."

I couldn't answer. I was still trying to get my head around the previous topic. I didn't know what I had done to deserve this. Dad had been following my strict instructions and keeping his distance but suddenly he was sprinting across the lawn to be by my side, like my knight in shining armour. Except he wasn't going to fight my corner. He just wanted to drag me away.

"My goodness, is that the time," he whispered in my ear. "We really ought to be going."

I ignored him.

"That's what you've been told," Liberty carried

on. "It's a story which has been spun like some sugar-coated fairy tale. But it's not true. It's a web of lies that your mum has woven around her past."

Tears welled up. Don't cry, I said to myself as a horrible dry scraping feeling in my throat made me want to gag.

"I don't know what you mean." I half choked on the words. "Mum and I don't have any secrets."

She laughed out loud. "Everyone has secrets, Laura, especially adults. How can you be so naive?"

"What are they then?"

Dad was beside himself now.

"Are you sure you want to know – to have the fairy tale shattered?" she continued.

"Yes," I shouted, "just tell me."

"No!" Dad's word whistled into my head so hard I'm surprised it didn't perforate my ear drum. "You don't want to listen to this, Laura. She doesn't know anything. Whatever she says will be lies and will just upset you."

It was his fault that it happened. He was in a panic, spinning around me, floating up in front of my face. I could feel his coldness, his fear rippling over me. I flailed my arms, trying to brush him away.

If Liberty had still been lying down in the hammock it would have been all right. I wouldn't have hit her square across the face. I saw her tilting backwards, tried to grab one of her outstretched arms, but I couldn't. Maybe Dad could have prevented her tipping over. Maybe he could have blown a huge gust of wind at her back, but he didn't. He let her fall. I heard her head *thud* against the ground, saw it jolt forwards and then back again. She just lay there. Eyes closed. Face completely white.

And me? For a second I was paralysed. I literally could not move, could not breathe. I honestly thought she was dead. And I had killed her.

TRUTH

I ran over and knelt down on the hard ground
scraped of grass from where people had constantly
climbed in and out of the hammock.

"Oh my God, Liberty. I didn't mean to do that."

She lifted her hand to the top of her head.

She was alive. I started to cry.

"I'm so sorry," I sobbed. "Are you all right?"

She opened her eyes. "Do I look all right?" she
mumbled.

"No. Don't move. I'll go and get your mum."

But when I turned around Aunt Jane was already
running across the grass.

"What on earth happened?" she shrieked.

I waited for Liberty to say that I pushed her off the
hammock. She looked at me but I couldn't work out
what her eyes were saying. Maybe she was concussed,
I thought. Maybe they weren't saying anything.

"Liberty, speak to me!" Aunt Jane obviously thought the same thing.

"I fell," she said at last.

I should have owned up, said it was all my fault. But I didn't. Things were difficult between Mum and Aunt Jane as it was. I couldn't bear to make it any worse.

"Does it hurt?" Aunt Jane asked.

"Yeah!" Liberty replied a bit sarcastically.

"Perhaps we should call an ambulance," I said.

Liberty sat up slowly with Aunt Jane supporting her back.

"No, it's not that bad," she said. "It sounded worse than it was."

"I'm so, so sorry," I mouthed as Aunt Jane supported her down the path and back inside the house.

I wanted to stay but Aunt Jane said Liberty needed to sit quietly for a while. "I'll ring later," I said, my hand on her arm.

"Fine," she said so quietly I almost couldn't hear it. Then, as I moved away, "Laura..."

"Yes?"

"What I said back there, about your mum and dad, just forget it. Please?"

I nodded. I'd have agreed to anything at that moment in return for an assurance that she was going to be okay.

"Don't worry about it, Lib. We all say things we don't mean."

"That was your fault," I said to Dad, as we walked back to the farm. "If you hadn't been flapping around, getting in my way, I wouldn't have lashed out."

He didn't say anything. In fact ever since Liberty fell flat on her back he'd been extremely quiet.

"Anyway," I said, shooting him a searching glance, "what was all that about you and Mum not being happy?"

Silence. Why did I get the feeling there was something he wanted to tell me?

"Dad?"

"I don't know why she said that."

"So it's not true?"

He stopped walking. So did I.

"Laura, I loved your mother. We had our moments

like all couples but I really loved her."

He paused and looked down at the pavement. "I don't know where Liberty's got her information from. Maybe your gran's been talking to her. I got the feeling that she was always hoping we wouldn't be happy so she could say, 'I told you so.'"

It was a plausible answer. All the same I got the feeling that it wasn't the whole truth. People can make up their own truth, can't they?

When I was six years old someone in my class had a fancy dress party. I was desperate to go to that party. I had my costume all ready. I was going to be Princess Jasmine from *Aladdin* and it was going to be such fun. Then I was ill. The night before I threw up and although the following morning I felt better, Mum wouldn't let me go to the party. I lay on the sofa and cried and cried, my princess dress and tiara thrown in a petulant heap onto my bedroom floor. Back at school everyone talked about that party for days and eventually I almost began to imagine that I'd been there. Years later I actually had to ask Mum whether I'd gone or not, whether it was not being allowed to go that

I'd made up.

If you are deliberately hiding something, though, you have to be very clever not to slip up eventually. I suppose, thinking about it, there had always been this feeling of secrecy in the family, the slightest of pauses, the tiniest of offbeat expressions when the past, our past, was mentioned. I hadn't wanted to pick up on it because I didn't want to disbelieve what Mum had told me and it would have meant that Gran might be bitter and vindictive towards Dad for a reason. I don't know why Liberty falling out of that hammock made me think differently but it was as if her bang on the head had affected me too. Suddenly I felt suspicious, as if everyone knew something that I didn't.

That night I lay in bed and looked at Dad asleep on my chair. I wanted to ask him to tell me the truth, the real truth, but the longer I lay there the more certain I was that he wouldn't. I began to wonder if anyone would. The following afternoon Mum asked me if I wanted to take a walk across the fields with her while Gran was resting. I did want to go and for us to spend some time together but there was something else preying on my mind. Something else that I wanted to do and for that I needed Mum *and* Dad out of the house.

So I was the one who insisted that someone should stay around in case Gran woke up and I managed to persuade Dad to go with Mum, making him promise that he wouldn't do anything weird that might freak her out. I watched from my bedroom window as they climbed over the fence. Even though Mum had no idea he was there, it was good to see them together.

As soon as I was sure that Mum wasn't going to turn around and come back to fetch something like a hat or her sunglasses or a bottle of water, I headed for her room. I didn't have long. I knew that it would only be a short walk. For a few moments I stood in the doorway, looking around. I felt really bad. I'm not a sneaky person and I respect other's people's privacy because I value my own but somewhere in Mum's bedroom I thought I might find a clue to what it was that everyone was hiding from me. Shame almost stopped me crossing the threshold but in the end I forced myself and started opening all the drawers and cupboards. My ribs

185

felt all constricted. Breath came in snatches. What if Mum came back and found me?

There was a shelf at the top of the wardrobe and my eyes settled on a dark wooden box that I didn't remember seeing before. I lifted it down and put it on the patchwork quilt covering the double bed. The top of the box was inlaid with an oval piece of mother of pearl and as I lifted the lid my heart beat a little faster. Inside were cards of condolence and beautiful handwritten letters, all going back to Dad's death. A car pulled into the yard and I leaped up to look out of the window, closing my eyes in relief as a man in overalls shouted to Uncle Pete. They wandered off towards the cowsheds and I scurried back to my task. Scanning the first few letters I felt my throat tighten, tears burn behind my eyes, so I sifted quickly through the rest, without reading them, and almost at the bottom I found something which made my hand pause in mid-air. Maybe this was what I was looking for – a note from cousin Penny. Slowly I picked it up and began to read:

Dear Liz,

I'm so sorry for everything that's happened. I feel partly

*responsible and if there's any way that I can make it up
to you please do not hesitate to let me know. You probably
don't feel like talking to me right now but if in the future
you or Laura need help, you know where I am.*

Take care of yourself, Liz.

With love,

Penny

I didn't understand what she was saying. It didn't
make sense. I read the letter several times, trying to
work out what was behind the words. But of course
I couldn't. The good news was that the letter had
been written on headed paper and Penny's address
was printed in navy block capitals at the top right
hand of the page. The date was a couple of weeks
after Dad died and, according to Mum, Penny had
moved house since then. All the same I scribbled
the name of the road and the postcode down on the
little pad of paper Mum kept next to her bed, tore
off the piece of paper, folded it up into a tight little
parcel and pushed it into my shorts pocket. I had no
idea what I was going to do with this information
but it seemed better than leaving the room with

nothing to go on. Maybe one day, if I could track her down, Penny would set everything straight.

* * *

It was a few days later when Liberty turned up in my room. She breezed in at ten o'clock on the dot and flung back my curtains. I was still asleep and not best pleased. In fact, I thought it was Dad messing about.

"Dad!" I groaned. "Give me a break, will you."

"Woo, spooky!" someone said. "You must be dreaming if you think I'm your dad."

I opened my eyes and blinked, glancing around the room for Dad. He wasn't there. Slowly I let out my breath and smiled. She smiled back, her eyes crinkling at the corners, her teeth stupendously straight and white. It was the first time I'd seen her since she fell out of the hammock, although I'd been texting every day to check she was all right and begging for forgiveness. I was so grateful that she hadn't snitched on me and I hadn't had to contend with Aunt Jane or Uncle Pete ranting and raging. Even though we hadn't met up, Lib kept texting back and assuring me that she was absolutely fine and as I propped myself up on one elbow, I could see she hadn't been lying. She was her usual glowing self.

"Lib, what are you doing here?"

She waved two little wicker baskets in front of my face, so close they almost touched my cheek.

"I thought you might like to go and collect the eggs together," she said, "like we used to."

"Yes," I said. "I'd like that."

"Great," she replied, chucking me a pair of shorts and a top. "You get dressed while I go and tell Gran what colour wool I want for the scarf she's promised to knit me."

And she went out leaving a sprinkling of happiness behind.

The orchard is right next to the vegetable patch and it was a Tuesday. Slowly, reluctantly, it began to dawn on me that maybe Liberty had an ulterior motive, that maybe her appearance was about more than collecting eggs. You really are getting suspicious of everyone, I said to myself.

But Liberty *did* flounce backwards and forwards a lot, and to me she seemed to laugh a bit too loudly every time she found an egg. Sam was working on the far side of the vegetable garden and the first time Liberty squealed as she stumbled into one of the hens' dustbowls he did look up, but apart from a brief wave he kept his head down. In the end she couldn't resist winging the odd flirtatious comment over to him. I cringed but although he was pretty quiet he didn't seem put off. Sometimes when boys really like you they get all tongue-tied and I reckoned that's why he was a bit shy with Liberty, either that or he was playing it cool.

Eventually I dragged her inside and we started to make fairy cakes with some of the eggs we'd collected, but she wasn't concentrating properly and had one eye looking out of the window all of the time. When Sam came inside to look through some seed catalogues with Gran I wondered if it was because he wanted to be close to Liberty. While he and Gran discussed the various types of vegetables to plant for the following year, Liberty giggled and shrieked as she got flour everywhere and cake mixture on the end of her nose. I just did my best to smile but I began to wish I hadn't suggested the baking at all.

"So," Sam said to Gran, "that's agreed then. We'll

have the Meteor broad beans again because they've been good this year and I'll sow some more lettuce to see you through the autumn."

"If I'm spared," Gran said, in overly dramatic tones.

"Of course you will be, Mrs G," Sam said. "You're needed here for a long while yet."

Gran liked that reply. I could tell. He just seemed to know all of the right things to say to her and having him around seemed to put Gran in a better mood.

Sam wasn't inside for that long and Liberty had to go home at twelve o'clock. Part of me wanted her to stay longer while I plucked up the courage to ask her what she'd meant when she'd talked about secrets and said that Mum and Dad weren't happy. But she had to go to the dentist and I was scared to bring things out into the open, scared that she'd get all angry again and I'd find out things I'd be better off not knowing. After she'd gone I slumped at the table, annoyed with myself for not tackling her. Gran let out an exaggerated sigh the minute Liberty shut the door behind her.

"Phew!" she said. "That young lady can be a bit over the top sometimes, can't she?"

I shrugged.

Gran looked out of the window.

"It looks very hot out there, Laura. Do you think you could take Sam a glass of water? I don't want him dehydrating."

"He's probably got a bottle with him," I replied.

"He might have drunk all of that," Gran persisted. "It'll only take you a couple of minutes."

"Yes, okay then," I sighed, "but I'm sure if he was thirsty he'd come and get his own water."

I waited for Gran to give me that disapproving look or bark out a rebuke for answering back. Instead she just picked up her knitting and *clickety-clacked* the needles together while I went and ran the tap.

He was bending over, picking some weeds out from between the lettuces. His checked shirt had come untucked and I could see the top of his turquoise boxer shorts. He turned around and I quickly looked up, my arm jerking as I held out the glass, water slopping over onto my hand.

"Gran thought you might want this."

He took it from me and downed the water in one go. A bit trickled down his chin and he wiped it with his sleeve. He smiled at me.

"Thanks. I needed that."

I swivelled on the spot, ready to make my escape. I felt annoyed with him and I didn't know why.

"Laura!"

"What?"

"Do you want come round to my house on Friday?" he asked as I stood with the sun blazing onto the crown of my head.

I paused. A bit too long. The silence sounded rude. And he was just trying to be nice. After all we were both a bit in the same boat. He was still settling in and I didn't exactly know stack-loads of people who I could socialise with.

"Yes, okay."

Aargh! Why did I do that? Sound so offhand sometimes, as if I couldn't care less. "Sorry, I meant yes. That would be good."

It's typical, isn't it? You don't do much for days and then suddenly you get two invitations at once.

Liberty texted me that evening, asking if I wanted to go to the cinema on Friday afternoon, because her mum could give us a lift into town. I had to say no and then she wanted to know why. She sounded really put out. I didn't want to lie but I didn't want to upset her by saying that I was meeting up with Sam so I made up some lame excuse about one of my friends from London who might be stopping off on her way for a weekend break with her parents. Then to add to my feelings of guilt there was Dad to deal with. He'd obviously been eavesdropping when I took the water out to Sam and had been in a bit of a mood for the rest of the day.

"I really don't like the way this is going, Laura," he said, pacing up and down in my room as I took my earrings out.

"He's a friend, Dad," I said, dropping the little silver flowers into the base of my jewellery tree. "That's all. And until I start school I need all the friends I can get."

But he didn't seem reassured and I had this horrible feeling that he was going to insist on coming with me again.

I had my first real row with Dad that Friday. It's not easy putting your point over when you can only whisper, in case someone else hears you. I knew there was going to be trouble almost as soon as I got up. I opened my chest of drawers and my wardrobe doors and wondered what to wear.

"What about that top?" Dad suggested, pointing to a brown T-shirt.

"Ugh no!" I replied. "It's really old and the neckline's all wrong. I don't know why I bought it."

"This one then."

"No, Dad. That one makes me look fat." I turned to look at him. "I know what you're trying to do."

"What?"

He opened his eyes really wide, trying for an expression of complete innocence. I wasn't fooled.

"You're trying to make me look hideous so Sam won't fancy me. But you really don't have to bother."

"No, I'm not. I wouldn't do such a thing and you could never look hideous."

"Yeah right, and I wouldn't eat a whole packet of double-chocolate-chip cookies if they were put in front of me."

I picked out a turquoise-blue T-shirt with a scooped neck and three little mother-of-pearl buttons on the front.

"You're not wearing that, are you?" Dad said, eyeing it suspiciously.

"Yes," I said, pushing the drawer closed in a definite way. "It's new so it'll make me feel nice."

He frowned disapprovingly. "It's quite low-cut. You'd better make sure those buttons are done up."

"Dad, for goodness' sake."

I plucked my jeans from the wardrobe and headed for the bathroom. He really could be a pain sometimes.

I was seeing Sam at three o'clock and after lunch Dad walked with me to the five-bar gate that led from the farmhouse onto the road. "You're not coming with me."

"Yes I am, young lady," he replied, head on one side, hand on hip.

"NO, YOU ARE NOT."

"And how are you going to stop me?"

That was a good question. I sighed, tried to run my fingers through my hair but they just got stuck in my curls and one of my nails snagged. Great!

"You need to give me some space, Dad. I can't handle all of this being followed, being watched all the time. It's as if I'm being stalked. It's doing my head in."

There, it was out in the open. I'd been thinking it for days but hadn't dared to say it.

"Well, I'm sorry," he snapped back, "and I thought that I was just being a responsible father, just trying to make up for lost time."

"And I feel as if you don't trust me. I feel as if I have to watch what I do and say all of the time in case you disapprove and I'm not the lovely Laura that you want me to be."

"Well I'm obviously not the father you want *me* to be."

We glared at each other.

"I didn't say that."

"As good as."

"Don't be childish."

"I'm not. If you don't want me around for your assignation then fine, I won't be. But if you get into trouble, if that boy tries it on, then don't expect me to make an appearance."

"Assignation?" I sort of laughed. "What sort of an expression is that?"

But he was fading now.

"I'm not having this discussion any longer," he said.

And with that he faded away. He'd got much better at that since he first appeared in my bedroom and made a hash of trying to hide from Mum. The trouble was that now I really didn't know if he was there or not. I leaned against the gate for a moment. *Wham!* The feeling hit me like one of Luke and Liam's footballs slamming straight into my stomach. Something had happened. Something big.

Don't get it out of proportion, Laura, I said to myself. It was just a row. All of those carefully constructed dreams about Dad, about what he was really like, how patient and understanding he would be, were ripped into ribbons. Finally I had to try and face up to it. Having Dad back in my life wasn't always as fantastic as I'd dreamed it would be.

Gloria

The front door to the vicarage was open, flooding the hall with light. Sunbeams bounced off the parquet floor. I rang the bell. Suddenly, stupidly, I felt nervous. Maybe Sam had just been trying to be nice. Maybe he really didn't want me here at all. After all he was a vicar's son. He was bound to have been brought up being kind to people and I was just one of them. I wasn't anyone special, not like Liberty. He probably wanted her to be standing here, not me. He was probably using me to get closer to her. But no, that's not what a nice, well-brought-up person would do. Aargh! I was so confused. I wanted to run away but a door banged off to the right and it was too late. Sam was already loping towards me.

"Hi," he said, quickly averting his eyes, "come in."

"Is it still okay? I mean I haven't got the wrong day or anything?"

He strode ahead and I almost had to run to keep up.

"No, why wouldn't it be?"

He flung the words over his shoulder and I suddenly wished that I'd got some company, that Dad had come with me after all. Having him there would have made me feel brave. Sam marched into the kitchen. I followed.

"Kettle's on," he said, turning to look at me, "and we've got a cake from one of the parishioners. Carrot, is that okay?"

"Great."

He clattered some mugs onto a tray while I perched on the arm of a pine bench, which was pushed back against the wall. He was all fingers and thumbs as he opened a tin and tried to separate two teabags. The shrillness of the whistle from the kettle seemed to match the atmosphere in the kitchen. He plonked the cake and two small plates onto the tray and gestured to me to follow him.

"I thought we'd be more comfortable in here."

The sitting room was rectangular with a large stone fireplace in the centre of one wall and patio doors at the far end. The curtains were pink velvet and a little bit faded but the room had a really homely, comfortable feel to it. Next to the sofa was a long, low bookshelf crammed with books and magazines and pots of pens. On top of it was a large vase painted with a peacock and lots of photographs in frames.

"It's no good," Sam said, almost dropping the tray onto the coffee table.

"What isn't?" I spluttered, wishing for the umpteenth time that I'd listened to Dad and stayed at home.

"Wait there," he said. "I really don't know whether I'm doing the right thing here and I need to know sooner rather than later."

He placed both palms over his cheeks. For some reason he couldn't look at me.

Oh my God, I thought and chastised myself for blaspheming in a vicarage. He's going to declare his undying love for Liberty. He's desperate to ask her out and wants to know where to take her on a date.

201

But then, instead of coming straight out with it, he told me to stay put while he went to get something. He frowned at me.

"You won't go away, will you?"

I shook my head. "Why would I?"

"You just look a bit... alarmed, that's all. There's no need to be. I'm not going to pounce on you or anything like that."

Part of me felt a sudden stab of disappointment.

"No... I mean... I didn't think that, not for one minute."

I could feel my face turning pink too. This was a disaster.

"I'll be back in a minute."

He darted off and I stood up, moving over to the window, trying to calm my nerves, which felt as if they were sticking out of me like porcupine needles. As I stared across the garden towards the fields full of sheep, who should appear, face pressed to the glass, but Dad. Having thought I'd be relieved to see him I actually felt furious.

"Are you all right?" he mouthed, his lips looking disconcertingly fishlike.

"Yes. Go away."

"You look nervous."

"That's because I never know these days when you're going to appear or disappear."

"I'm only looking out for you, Laura."

"And putting thoughts into my head that weren't there before. Now go away. Please."

How many times did I have to tell him? He frowned but he began to fade.

"You'd better have gone," I mouthed, staring into the garden, trying to spot the slightest sign of him. It was very still outside, even the delphiniums in the border weren't waving about, so I turned around and wandered across the room to look at the photos of Sam. Concentrating on something might stop my heart from beating so fast and ease that tight, breathless feeling in my chest. Some of the photos were of Sam with his mum and dad. There was one with his sister and a beautiful arty black and white one of his mum with the two of them. Eventually I sat bolt upright on the sofa, in exactly the place I had been before Sam left the room. The fingers of one hand pulled at the fringing on the cushion beneath me. On the mantelpiece a rectangular-shaped clock in a wooden case chimed the half hour. Sam was back in less than two minutes but it seemed much longer. I half turned as he came into the room.

"Don't look around," he instructed. "In fact, close your eyes." He was standing right behind me. It was really hard to keep my eyes closed. They wanted to flutter open, to give me the safety of sight.

He leaned over the back of the sofa so his face was very close to mine. If I'd turned our lips would have touched. He placed something on my lap, something soft and stumbling.

"You can open your eyes now."

I didn't need to open my eyes to know what it was. I didn't need to see the tiny, fluffy ball of stripy black and brown fur to know that this was what I had longed for, for nearly all of my life. She turned towards me and I was lost in the huge, deep-blue eyes looking up at my face. This, I thought, must be what it's like to be in love.

"Oh!" I gasped.

I lifted the kitten up to my face and touched her nose with mine.

"Hello," I whispered. "What's your name?"

She squirmed in my hands but a tiny pink tongue came out and licked my cheek.

I laughed and kissed the top of her head.

"Is she yours?" I asked Sam, unable to tear my gaze away from her.

"She's a present," he said.

The pain that shot through me was like a searing burn, more intense than anything I'd ever felt before.

"For Liberty?"

He frowned. "No, not for Liberty. Why would it be for her?"

"I just thought…"

He took a deep breath.

"The kitten is for you, Laura."

"For me?"

My head was swimming. I felt completely disconnected from reality. I barely knew this boy and he had done this, for me. Suddenly, all of the disappointments, all of the hurts of the last few weeks and months had been flung away.

"Really?" I asked, almost struck dumb with disbelief.

"Yes, really." He smiled, leaning over and tickling the kitten behind her ears. "She's all yours. If you want her. I didn't mean to make you cry."

Sam grabbed a box of tissues from the coffee table, shoved a clump into my hand and sat down beside me. I dabbed at my eyes, wishing I hadn't bothered with mascara as it was probably all running down my cheeks.

"I'm sorry." My voice sort of cracked in two.

"If you don't want her, I can probably find someone else who does."

I held the kitten close, felt her tiny heart beating against mine as I bent my head and rested my chin between her ears.

"Of course I want her," I murmured. "How could anyone not want her? She's gorgeous."

"Phew!" He wiped a hand theatrically across his brow.

I lifted the kitten up to my face and rested her against my shoulder.

"The problem is, I don't know if I'll be allowed to keep her. In London, Mum always said no to pets. I had a goldfish once, which Dad won from the fair just before he died but that's it. And then there's Gran. We're living in her house and I know she used to have cats but…"

"Your gran knows, Laura. It was partly her idea. I mentioned that one of Dad's parishioners in the next village had a kitten going spare and that you'd said how you'd always wanted a cat. Your gran's cool about it."

I smiled at the word. Only a few weeks ago I wouldn't have been able to imagine Gran being cool about anything, let alone anything to do with me.

"And Mum…?"

"Your gran's talked her round. I think your mum's just pleased to see your gran so enthusiastic about something for a change. She thinks it might be good for both of you."

The kitten flopped against my shoulder like a baby.

"You've all been plotting behind my back."

He grinned. "Yep!"

"It's one of the nicest things anyone has ever done for me. Thank you."

And I leaned over and kissed him on the cheek. He looked embarrassed but not in a totally dismayed way. I laughed and so did he.

"I couldn't sleep last night," he said. "I was worried that I'd made a big mistake. Lots of people say they want things but when it comes to it they change their mind."

"I know," I said, "but I haven't changed my mind about this. No way."

"Good," he said, passing me my mug of tea. "What are you going to call her?"

"I've no idea."

I held the wriggling kitten out in front of me.

"What shall I call you?" I asked.

She opened her mouth and mewled.

"Something pretty, you say?"

I turned towards Sam.

"*You* should name her," I said, "after all, you got her for me."

"Uh huh!" he said, shaking his head. "You can't duck out of it like that. She's yours. You've got to choose the name."

So we spent the rest of the afternoon trying to think up names and in the end it was right in front of me – or rather to the side of me. In the bookshelves were loads of CDs and on top of a higgledy-piggledy pile was one by Johann Sebastian Bach. Right across the front in big yellow letters it said 'Gloria in excelsis Deo'. That had been one of Grandad's favourite pieces of music. He played it all the time. He even played it to the cows because he said it helped them to produce more milk.

"Gloria!" I said to Sam. "I'm going to call her Gloria."

"Wow! That sounds awesome. Where did you get that from?" he asked.

I picked up the CD and waved it in front of him.

"From here and from my grandad."

Sam tickled the kitten under her chin.

"I like it," he said. "It's perfect."

I beamed at him. I couldn't believe that I could feel so happy.

COMPLICATIONS

"You might as well show yourself because I know you're there," I said as I made my way home.

Dad slunk out from behind a row of conifers.

"Have you been spying on me?"

He did have the grace to look shamefaced.

"Not all of the time," he replied. "What's that you're carrying?" I clutched the cardboard box close to my chest.

"It's a present from Sam."

"Oh yes?" He sounded suspicious.

"Don't be like that. It's one of the best things anyone's ever given me."

He raised an eyebrow, trying to look nonchalant, but I could tell that he was burning up with curiosity. So he *was* telling the truth. He really hadn't been watching me all of the time. Maybe my message was beginning to get through after all. I stopped, sat on a low stone wall and put the box on my lap.

"Do you want a peek?"

The chance of him saying no was absolutely zilch.

I opened the top of the box.

"What on earth is that?" Dad spluttered as Gloria mewled a greeting.

"I'd have thought that was obvious," I replied. "I've called her Gloria. Isn't she gorgeous?"

Dad had taken one look and then several paces back.

"What's the matter? Don't you like her?"

He had his hand clasped over his mouth and nose.

"She's a cat!"

"Well spotted."

"Cats don't like me."

"Don't be silly. She's only a little kitten and she's never met you before. She doesn't know not to like you."

"No, I don't mean that. What I mean is – I'm allergic to them."

"Oh!"

All sorts of thoughts raced through my mind but I didn't think it would be a real problem.

After all, Dad was a ghost, not a human. Just because he was allergic to cats in a previous life didn't mean that he would be now, did it? And then he sneezed, several times. It was a real man sneeze and Gloria almost jumped out of the box. An elderly lady on the other side of the road gave me a funny look. I turned away and smoothed Gloria's spiked-up fur.

"We'll be home soon and you can come out of there," I said to her before closing her in.

"No!" Dad was quite emphatic. "You can't keep her."

"I'm sorry?" I couldn't believe what I was hearing.

"You can't keep her, Laura. Not if you want me to stay around."

I gasped. "That's blackmail."

He didn't reply, just stared at his feet.

"How can you say that?" I demanded. "Don't you want me to be happy?"

"Of course I want you to be happy. You know that I want that more than anything in the whole world."

"Well it doesn't seem like it right now."

He stood very still. His edges didn't ripple at all. His face was like a mask.

"Stop ignoring me," I said, kicking out. I was only trying to make gentle contact with his aura but instead I hit his leg. I saw my foot go straight through it and at almost the same time he leaped in the air.

"Ouch!"

He held his foot in his hand and hopped around. It was totally over the top.

"I'm sorry. I didn't mean to kick you and I didn't know it would hurt – but you shouldn't have blanked me like that."

He looked upset. "It just feels as if you'd rather have the kitten than me."

Gloria was scrabbling away at the box, getting distressed. I couldn't stay here, standing in the street with her.

"I never thought I'd have to make a choice. Before Sam gave her to me I'd have said that I might have problems with Mum or Gran – but not with you."

"Well, things don't always turn out the way you expect them to," he said softly, so softly that I hardly heard the words.

He lifted his head.

"I hate to say this, Laura, but I can't stay around if you keep the kitten."

I stared at him.

"You don't mean that."

My heart felt as if someone had sawn straight into it with a jagged knife. But he wasn't going to budge. I could tell from the set expression on his face. I clutched the box to me. It wasn't fair. He wasn't being fair. I hated him, really hated him in that moment but, at the same time, all those years of love, of wanting him around were swelling up and swamping me. I couldn't risk losing him now. So I turned around and headed straight back to the vicarage with tears streaming.

"Laura, let me in."

Mum pushed against the door but I'd dragged the chest of drawers in front of it and barricaded myself in my room.

"I'm fine."

"No, you're obviously not."

The chest of drawers slid slightly on the bare boards as the door opened by about ten centimetres.

"I don't want to talk about it."

There was a long pause but I knew Mum was still outside the door. I could almost hear her thought processes as she wondered what to do for the best.

"All right," she said at last. "If that's the way you feel. I'll be in the garden if you change your mind."

I heard the creak on the top step of the stairs as she left me alone. I knew exactly what she was going to do next. She was going to ring Sam and find out what had happened. She and Gran were expecting a kitten. Where was it? What had gone wrong? I couldn't explain, could I?

They had been waiting for me when I got back to the farm, their faces full of anticipation and excitement. In front of the range there was a snug little drawer lined with a pink blanket and, in a corner of the kitchen,

215

a brand new bowl with paw prints painted on the front. I'd seen them through a blur.

Mum had been waiting for me so there was no escape. She'd sat me at the kitchen table briefly and tried to find out what had gone wrong. Eventually I escaped to my room and blocked myself in – or, in actual fact, tried to block other people out. It was pointless of course. The one person I was trying to keep out was Dad and no amount of piled-up furniture would do that, not that he was coming anywhere near me at that moment. Even he seemed to show some sensitivity and realise when he wasn't wanted. I cried myself to sleep and when I woke up my whole face ached. It was as if it had been screwed up like a piece of scrap paper and then someone had tried unsuccessfully to smooth it out again. I sat up and moved to the dressing table. I looked awful, puffy and blotchy. Downstairs I could hear the signature tune of the evening news on the television. There was the vague aroma of something cooking too. Life was carrying on as normal, which just made me feel worse.

I pulled the chest of drawers away from the door

intending to wash my face in the bathroom. My skin felt tight where the tears had dried in vertical strips like Scotch tape. As I stepped out onto the landing I got a shock. Gran was sitting right outside my room, ramrod straight in the high ladder-backed chair.

"Gran, what are you doing there? How did you get upstairs?"

"I'm waiting for you, Laura, and it's amazing what you can do when you put your mind to it."

She looked around, as if searching for something, before turning back to me.

"Can we talk?"

"What about?"

"About why you took that kitten back to Sam."

I shook my head. "It's complicated."

"Life generally is, sweetheart."

I blinked. The last thing I wanted was someone being kind to me, especially Gran. But she reached out and took hold of my hand, examined my fingers.

"I want you to know, Laura, that I'm here for you. If you need me, if you want someone to talk to, I've got plenty of time to listen, in confidence."

I stared at her, wondering exactly what she was trying to convey. Now it was my turn to look around, to see if Dad was lurking somewhere, listening.

"Thank you," I whispered. "But I can't explain about the kitten. I just can't. I'm sorry."

Gran looked at me, long and hard. "What about me?" she asked. "What if *I* wanted the kitten? Would that be all right?"

"No," I whispered, "I don't think it would. It might trip you up or claw at your furniture or…" I felt the tears start again.

"Let's leave this conversation for now," Gran said, stroking my hand. "Go and wash your face and come downstairs for some supper. Your mother's made a lasagne."

"Did she speak to Sam?"

"Yes."

"I bet he hates me. I bet he thinks I'm completely screwed up."

"I'm sure he doesn't think any such thing," Gran said.

"Well I hate myself," I said.

"That's just silly, and feeling sorry for yourself won't solve this problem."

"I won't change my mind."

Gran stood up slowly and made her way to the top of the stairs. She leaned heavily on the banisters, shaking away my offer of help.

"Actually, the kitten is not the problem I was referring to," she murmured and she concentrated very hard on putting her feet firmly on each step.

I watched her descend, one careful footstep after the other, until she reached the bottom.

She knows about Dad, I thought to myself. Or at least she suspects. And suddenly this massive sense of foreboding dropped over me like some dark, heavy piece of material.

CONSEQUENCES

I didn't know what to do, who to turn to. If Gran knew about Dad there was one thing I was absolutely certain of – she wouldn't want him to stay here. She'd be determined to get rid of him. I hadn't seen him since I'd barricaded myself in my room. I kept expecting him to appear, to comfort me. I half hoped that he'd beg my forgiveness and say that he'd changed his mind. But he didn't. He steered clear. As soon as I was sure that Gran was out of earshot I went back into my bedroom.

"Dad?" I called softly. "Are you there? You've got to come out. I need to talk to you."

Silence except for a hedge trimmer whining in the distance.

I banged my hand on the windowsill.

"I thought you heard me when I called you.

I thought you said you'd always be there if I needed you. You're a liar."

That did it. He materialised in the corner of the room, his forehead wrinkled by a frown and his lips set in a stubborn line.

"It's not nice to call someone a liar, Laura. What's the matter?"

"It's Gran!"

He groaned. "The bane of my life and my death."

"She knows about you."

"You've told her?" He looked incredulous.

"No, of course not. Have you appeared to her? You said when you first arrived that you might do that."

"Well I haven't, so I have no idea how she's cottoned on. Are you sure?"

I nodded. His frown deepened. His eyes seemed to darken.

"She'd want to get rid of me, wouldn't she?"

"Afraid so."

We were on the same wavelength. I could almost see the thoughts whirling around in his head.

"I don't want to leave you, Laura."

I bit my lip. Hard.

"Can you go away for a little while and then come back?"

He shook his head. "I don't think so. I'm not sure. What if I make the return journey and then can't get back to see you for ages – or maybe not at all? I can't take that risk."

Despite the fact that I was cross with him I wanted to hug him, to hold on to him, to tell him that I never wanted to let him go again either. Instead I tried to be practical and not to let my emotions run away with me.

"You'll have to keep a low profile for a few days," I said. "No icy draughts as you waft through the house. In fact, maybe you'd better not be in the house at all. You could stay in one of the outbuildings for a while."

He pulled a face.

I must have looked exasperated because he threw his hands up in the air as if in surrender.

"All right, if that's what you want. I'll do my best but I'm sure everything's going to be fine."

Except it wasn't, for loads of reasons. I hadn't

heard from Sam since taking the kitten back. I hadn't even been able to bring myself to look in the box. I'd just whispered, "Goodbye and good luck," to Gloria before depositing the box back in Sam's arms without a rational explanation. I didn't want to go out in case I bumped into him and he started asking awkward questions or, even worse, blanked me. So I stayed mostly around the house with the odd trip over to the hay barn where Dad had set up camp. I felt on edge, as if Gran was watching my every move. Then her tablets went missing and as Mum and I hunted all over the house Gran made some comment about 'strange things happening'.

"You remember when that photograph moved?" she said to Mum.

"Yes, yes," Mum said distractedly.

"Well maybe whoever or whatever did that has taken my tablets."

Gran didn't look at me but I knew exactly what she meant. Mum stood up and looked at both of us.

"It wasn't me who moved the photograph," I protested.

Mum shook her head and threw a couple of

cushions back on the sofa in a random way. I knew what she was thinking – that Gran was going senile.

"Perhaps you put them down outside," I said to Gran and at the first opportunity I slipped out of the back door, across the farmyard and into the barn.

"Psst, Dad," I whispered, checking that Uncle Pete was still tinkering about with his tractor on the other side of the yard. "Come out. I need to ask you something."

He poked his head out from around the corner of a hay bale.

"Gran's lost her tablets. Did you take them?"

"No, of course not." He sounded a bit indignant.

"Well they've gone missing and we can't find them anywhere."

"So you think it's me?" He looked hurt now.

"I just thought that you might be a bit annoyed at having to move out here and…"

"Laura, I wouldn't do something like that. She's probably put them down somewhere and forgotten about it."

I felt really bad for accusing him.

"I'm sorry. It's just so tense in there." I tilted my

head towards the house. "Mum and Aunt Jane are still bickering, Liberty's making herself unavailable and Gran's watching me like a hawk."

He stood in front of me and blew a kiss on to my forehead. "It's just taking time for things to settle down, that's all. You've all had big changes to adjust to. Your mum's lost her job, moved house and is now looking after your gran. It's not easy for anyone. Things will get better."

I smiled. "What are you now, some fortune teller?"

"No, just someone who knows that you are all kind and sensible people who can make this work. Now why don't I come and give you a hand looking for these tablets?"

So we walked back over to the house together and I felt reassured by Dad's words. In the end it was him who found the tablets, in the pantry, next to the sugar.

"Oh!" Gran said. "I must have put them down when I got up to make myself a cup of tea in the night. Silly me. I'm getting so forgetful."

Suddenly she looked close to tears.

"I'm nothing but trouble these days."

Mum dropped a hand on to Gran's shoulder. "Don't upset yourself, Mother. It's all sorted now."

Two days after that, Gran and I were sitting watching television together. Mum had gone out for a drink at the pub with Sam's dad. He'd been around to visit Gran a few times and Mum seemed to like talking to him too. In fact, I began to wonder if he was really just coming to see Gran. I think she did too. I was just hoping that Mum would find out about Gloria and if she had a nice new home to go to, when an orange rolled through the slightly open door. It came to a stop just beneath Gran's feet. For a minute or so I thought that she hadn't seen it. I was about to reach down and pick it up when she turned her eyes from the television and looked straight at me.

"Where did that come from?" she asked.

"I've no idea," I lied. Dad was just outside the sitting room door, beckoning to me.

"Laura," he mouthed. "I want to talk to you."

I stood up. Gran was quiet for a moment.

"I could have fallen over that," she murmured,

226

"and seriously hurt myself. Is that what he wants? To finish me off?"

I felt all of the energy draining out of me.

"Who?"

My voice was so weak but perhaps it was because Gran, despite the quietness of her voice, suddenly sounded and looked so much stronger in herself.

"Your father, Laura. That's who I'm talking about."

I judged it was better to say nothing. To be honest I didn't know what to say.

"I haven't lived in this house for all of these years, not to know when there's something funny going on."

She looked around the room.

"Is he here now? Can you see him?"

I glanced over to the door, not knowing what to do or say. Dad was sitting back on his haunches mouthing, "Sorry." Immediately Gran followed my gaze. I hadn't intended to but I'd given him away. Actually no, that's wrong. He'd given himself away by rolling that stupid orange.

Oh, Dad, I thought, as he sloped off into the shadows. You don't know what you've done.

"He can't stay, Laura. He doesn't belong here."

Keep silent, I said to myself. If you don't speak, you can't say anything incriminating. Dad had blended into the shadows of the hall now. Gran struggled to her feet and waved her stick in the air.

"I know you're here, Gareth, and you're not welcome. This is my house, not yours. I don't want you here. Haven't you caused enough trouble in life without coming back? GO AWAY!"

"Mother! Laura! What's going on? What on earth are you doing?"

Mum stood in the doorway staring at Gran as if she thought she'd completely flipped. Gran stood so still I thought she might have died on the spot. Then she began to wobble. I took her arm and she leaned heavily against me. She began to tremble and I tightened my grip.

"We were playing a game," I said to Mum, my brain scrabbling for an explanation that she would believe. "Gran was showing me what she'd do if she thought the house was haunted."

"Which it isn't," Gran said, a bit too quickly.

"But you mentioned Gareth's name," Mum said.

"Oh no!" Gran replied, her features rearranging themselves into a picture of innocence. "You must have misheard, dear."

Mum looked at me.

I shook my head, shrugged my shoulders. "Don't think so, Mum."

She stared at me. For a moment I thought she was going to dig deeper but we must have made a convincing team, Gran and I, because Mum plonked herself down in the chair and just let it go.

"How extraordinary that you should be talking about ghosts," she said. "Sam's dad and I have been discussing the same thing. It turns out that we've got our very own ghostbuster on the doorstep. The vicar is part of the Diocesan Deliverance Team which deals with 'unwelcome spiritual visitors'. Did you know that, Laura?"

"No," I whispered, "no, I didn't."

"So," Mum said, picking up the orange which I had left on the table, rolling it between her hands, "if we ever *do* get any trouble of that kind, we

229

know just where to go, don't we?"

I didn't look at Gran. I didn't dare. But I had a good idea that I knew exactly what she was thinking.

"Dad," I said later when I was in my bedroom and I heard Mum running the bath, "will you PLEASE make an appearance. I need to talk to you face to face."

He materialised sitting in the chair.

"You're in big trouble," I said. "Why on earth did you roll that orange?"

"I was trying to get your attention. You'd told me to be careful so I wanted to stay outside the room."

"What was so urgent that it couldn't wait?"

He shrugged, looked a little upset.

"I wanted to talk about your mother. You know she's seeing that man."

"If you mean the vicar, they're just friends."

"Huh!" he said with a whoosh which nearly blew all my random bits of paper off my bedside table. "I don't think so."

"You're jealous!"

His foot toyed with the fringe on the edge of the rug.

"Dad, Mum is entitled to go out with people. You've been dead for ten years. You can't expect her to stay single for ever."

He didn't reply.

"Don't you want her to be happy too?"

He looked up then. "Of course I do. It's just…
difficult, seeing her with someone else."

"She's hardly been out with anyone since you
died. He seems like a nice, kind man."

He nodded. "You're right. But it still hurts."

"You do realise that Gran's going to talk to the
Reverend Tim about you? And then he'll come
around and ring bells and wave incense or whatever
it is they do. Anyway basically he'll get rid of you,
send you back to where you came from."

He didn't look that concerned. "Maybe that
would be for the best. Maybe it's too upsetting for
everyone, me being here."

"You don't mean that," I replied. "I think you
need to go away from here for a while, just until
things settle down."

"Like where?"

"I don't know, take a holiday or something,
go back to The Other Side, just temporarily."

"I told you, it's not as easy as that."

"Well we've got to do something. What about Cousin Penny? Could you stay with her for a while? Maybe she's got a spare bedroom you could hole up in."

"I'd rather stay here with you."

"And I'd rather have you here," I said.

"Let's wait," he said. "All of this will probably blow over and your gran will forget all about it."

I stared at him. If he thought that Gran would let this go he really was deluding himself. I knew that once Gran got her teeth into something there was no way she was going to let it drop.

I was just coming out of my bedroom the next morning when I heard her on the phone. From the landing window I could see Mum hanging out washing in the garden.

"We need some help," she said.

I paused, crouching by the banisters to hear her voice more clearly. "We have an unwanted presence in the house and it needs to be dealt with. Liz said that you can arrange that sort of thing."

She was obviously talking to the vicar but from

the tone of her voice you'd have thought that she was arranging an assassination – which in a way she was.

"Oh yes," Gran continued. "I know exactly who it is."

There was a pause as the person at the other end spoke.

"All right," Gran said, at last. "I'll wait to hear from you with a time but can you try to make it sooner rather than later? And Tim," she added, "I'd rather Liz didn't know about this for now. Can we just keep it between ourselves? I don't want her to be upset."

Another pause as the vicar spoke.

"Oh, Laura knows," Gran said. "I suspect that Laura's the reason he's come back. She's always had this rather gilded view of her father. That's partly Liz's fault. I suspect that the entity we are talking about…"

I shook my head. Even after all these years she still could barely bring herself to call Dad by his name.

"… I suspect he's getting a bit twitchy that

233

Laura might find out the truth because, I can tell you, Tim, that man was not the honourable, devoted father and husband that she thinks he was."

I got pins and needles in my foot, moved a smidgeon, but the floorboard beneath me still creaked. I saw Gran's shadow on the wall shift as she looked upwards.

"I've got to go," she whispered. "I'll wait to hear from you. Thank goodness you are here, Tim. I feel so much better for talking to you. Bye."

She put the phone down and I listened to her walk back to the kitchen. Was I imagining it or was she not leaning on her stick quite so much? Was there almost a spring in her step?

I stayed where I was, trying to absorb what I had heard. All those weeks of Gran and I growing closer seemed to have been wiped away with a few words: 'that man was not the honourable, devoted father that she thinks he was'.

How dare she say that! How dare she make arrangements to get rid of *my* dad without even consulting me! One thing was for sure. While there was breath in my body I was not going to let it happen.

DESPERATION

I had no idea how much time I had. The vicar could have been around the following day or not for a couple of weeks. I concocted my plan that morning and I didn't tell anyone, especially not Dad. Every day at around lunchtime he took himself off for a drift around the village so I was pretty sure as Mum, Gran and I sat in the garden, eating sandwiches, that he wasn't around.

"Mum," I asked, "can I go to London tomorrow? Abi has texted me. It's her birthday and some of my friends are getting together."

"It's a bit short notice," Mum said.

"Oh, let her go," Gran said. "It'll do her good to get away from here and catch up with her old friends."

Did Gran want me out of the way tomorrow or was I being paranoid? Had the vicar phoned back

 235

and arranged to exterminate Dad that soon? Was I acting just in the nick of time?

"It'll just be for the day," I said, trying to quell the sudden wobble in my voice, "although Abi said I could stay the night if I wanted to."

I'm not a good liar. I was sure Mum would see through me but she didn't. Maybe it was because Gran was making such a big thing of letting me go. At least I could be grateful to her for that.

The following morning I got up early and packed a small rucksack.

"Where are you going?" Dad asked, wandering into my bedroom.

"To London. You shouldn't be in the house. It's safer in the barn."

"It's lonely out there. What are you going to London for?"

"To meet up with some friends."

I felt in the back pocket of my jeans for the small piece of paper that was vital to my plan, although to be honest I didn't really need it. I had memorised Penny's old address. I just hoped that if I went to her previous house I could track her down.

"Is Liberty going with you?"

"No."

"What about that boy?"

"If you mean Sam, you know that I haven't seen him since I handed the kitten back.' That wasn't strictly true. I *had* seen him in the distance, walking down the road with Liberty welded to his side. It had choked me up; still did. They looked like an item and even though that bit of information would have made Dad happy, I couldn't bring myself to tell him. 'Sam even made an excuse to get out of doing the gardening last week. I don't suppose he'll even want to share the same air as me on the school bus when term starts, let alone spend a whole day with me in London."

"I didn't mean to spoil things, Laura. I just didn't think that the kitten was a good idea. Maybe I was wrong."

"It's a bit late to say that now," I gasped.

"So you're going on your own?" he persevered.

"Yes. Anything wrong with that?"

"Oh my goodness," he shrieked, "hundreds, no,

237

thousands of things. What *is* your mother thinking of?"

"Dad, I'm quite capable of getting on a train and navigating the Tube by myself."

I paused to let all the ramifications of that sink in. I could see the worry etched across his face. My plan was working perfectly. I'd dangled the fishing line in front of him, now to reel it in.

"Why don't you come with me, if you're really worried?"

He stared at me. For a second I thought he wasn't going to take the bait.

"You wouldn't mind?"

I knew that I couldn't say no. He wasn't stupid and would definitely suspect something was up if I did that.

"Well, yes I would." I paused. "But if you are going to come I'd rather it was all upfront, instead of spotting you lurking in the distance, like some inept spy. Actually, considering you're a ghost you're not that good at following me without being unobserved."

He chewed at his bottom lip. "To be fair you *are* getting better at spotting when I'm around."

He mulled over my suggestion.

"I'm being overprotective, aren't I?" he said, at

last. "It's probably better if I stay here."

I tried not to look dismayed, tried my best to look relieved, happy even, but inside I was furious.

All this time I'd been trying to get that message over and now, just when I didn't want him to, he'd chosen to take it on board. Parents can be so irritating sometimes.

"You don't want me looking over your shoulder all the time. I can see that now. You go off and have a nice day with your friends without me hanging around."

He meant it. He really meant it! What on earth was I going to do now?

"Laura!" Mum called up the stairs. "Are you ready? You're going to miss your train."

"Yes, coming," I shouted.

I didn't know what to do. He HAD to come with me. I had to get him away from there.

I stood looking around my room, trying to think of something, anything.

"Laura!" Mum flung open the door now. "What are you doing in here? You know how I hate rushing. You're going to be running along the platform at this rate."

"I can always get the next train," I said. "Do you think I need my umbrella?"

"No, you can't," she said. "You're booked on a specific train and you have to get that one unless you want to pay a lot more. Now come on. You don't need your umbrella."

Out of the corner of my eye I could see Dad beginning to get a bit twitchy.

"I can't find my phone," I lied. "I can't go without my phone. I won't be able to get in touch with you to let you know I've arrived safely."

"Well where did you last have it?" she huffed, pulling back my duvet and scanning the room. "It's not like you to lose things."

"It must be around somewhere," I said.

Mum checked her watch. "You'll have to take mine."

"It's okay. I'll go without it. I can ring you from Abi's phone."

"No, Laura," Dad hissed in my ear. "Take your mother's phone. What if you get separated from Abi? What if you get lost or mugged? You need to have a phone."

I waved him away and grabbed the rucksack.

"It'll be fine," I whispered as I followed Mum down the stairs. "To be perfectly honest you're more likely to get mugged *for* your phone in London these days. It's probably safer without one."

"Oh my God!" He was rippling with anxiety now.

"It'll be fine. Don't worry."

"No," he said, "I've changed my mind. I'd better come with you. I shall be a nervous wreck if I stay here imagining what's happening to you."

RESULT!

I wanted to skip out to the car but of course I didn't. I assumed my very best put-upon expression and just said one word. "Whatever!"

The train was pretty full so Dad had to sit a little way away from me. I was quite glad. I didn't want to have to take part in a surreptitious conversation.

"So, where's your friend Abi?" Dad asked as we went through the barrier at St Pancras station. "I thought she was meeting you here."

"Oh, it wasn't definite. She said that if she couldn't make it to meet up at her house."

"Oh, Laura," Dad gasped. "I knew something would go wrong. It's such a good thing that I came with you, isn't it?"

I just looked at him and smiled. Little do you know, I thought, how much of a good thing it is.

I'd already studied the Tube map so I knew just where I was going. We pushed our way through the throng of people and hopped on the Underground. It was really hot down there and I was glad to get out into the fresh air. I was beginning to panic a bit. What if I couldn't track down Penny? What if Dad wouldn't agree to stay with her for a while? I stood outside the station and studied my *A–Z* map while Dad looked up and down the street.

"I miss this," he said. "Derbyshire's all right for a short time but this is where the action is."

"So you wouldn't mind staying here then?" I asked, setting off in what I hoped was the right direction.

"No, I'd love it," Dad said. I turned into a long straight road with villa-type houses on either side.

"This looks familiar," Dad said. "Where did you say your friend Abi lived?"

"All roads in London look similar," I replied,

walking a little quicker, hoping to get to No. 65 before he cottoned on to what I was doing. It had a number made of pieces of mosaic tile and a little porch with white painted spindles above a black and white tiled floor. Two stone pots of red geraniums stood next to the front door. It looked like a nice house. I walked up the path, took a deep breath and rang the bell.

"Are you sure your friend Abi lives here?" Dad asked.

He was still standing on the pavement, looking up at the house. Inside the house, I heard the jangle of keys and through the obscured glass in the top of the door I could see someone moving towards me.

"Dad, I'll explain in a minute."

"Explain what? Laura, what are you up to?"

The door opened and a woman of about forty stood in front of me. She wore a purple flowery blouse and white jeans. Her hair was curly and mid-brown but with blond bits at the ends.

"I'm sorry to disturb you," I said. "But I'm looking for someone who used to live here."

She didn't speak, just looked rather surprised,

alarmed even. My heart was hammering away in my chest.

"Her name's Penny," I hesitated. How stupid. I didn't even know her surname. "I'm sorry, this was a really bad idea."

I felt the tears spring up behind my eyes. My chest was tight. I turned to go. Dad was blocking my exit as I floundered down the path, head down.

"Laura!"

I stopped and turned to look at the woman through bleary eyes.

"It is Laura, isn't it?"

I nodded as she padded down the path in bare feet and took my arm.

"I'm Penny," she said. "You'd better come in and tell me what this is about."

"No! No! No!" Dad muttered in my ear.

But it was too late. Penny was steering me through the front door. Behind me I was aware of Dad clutching his head in his hands and then him sprinting to get through the door before Penny shut it. Poor Dad! He looked horrified. I so wanted to tell him that I was doing this for his own good.

SANCTUARY

Penny gestured to a two-seater sofa in the kitchen. I sank onto the grey velvet and leaned back against brightly coloured felt cushions. Dad hovered in the doorway.

"Would you like a drink?" she asked.

I nodded.

"Tea, coffee, something cold?"

"Just water will be fine," I whispered.

She got two glasses from a cupboard and filled them to the brim, before sitting down next to me. I sipped at the water. I wasn't thirsty. It was just something to do, to buy time. She had this calmness about her as she sat, quietly watching me with her cool grey eyes.

"How did you know who I was?" I asked at last.

She smiled slightly. "I knew exactly who you

 245

were the minute I opened the door. You look just like your father."

"Really?"

I looked over at Dad who was running his fingers through his hair. So far as I could see that was where our resemblance ended.

"Really," she replied, leaning back a little as if to study me even better. "Does your mother know that you're here?"

I wanted to just say yes, not to complicate things, but there was something about this woman that made me feel bad about lying. Besides, she was studying me so intently I wasn't sure I'd be able to pull off a lie without giving myself away.

"She knows that I'm in London."

"I see."

She got up, opened a packet of biscuits and arranged them on a small yellow vintage plate splattered with little green clover leaves. Then she came back and sat down beside me again. I took a biscuit. It was a ginger nut and cracked as I bit into it. The sound seemed to echo around the inside of my head.

"So what can I do for you, Laura? Why did

you want to find me?"

I stared at the crumbs that had fallen into my lap. How on earth could I answer that?

"I heard you'd moved to Derbyshire?" Penny said when I didn't answer her question.

"Yes. Gran had a fall and Mum lost her job and..." I shrugged, "... she decided that she needed a change."

"And is it okay, living in Derbyshire? Are you happy?"

"I didn't want to move. I didn't want to leave the grave. But I knew that you'd look after it. You will look after it, won't you? I mean, we've only been gone for a few weeks but I like it to have fresh flowers."

I looked out of her window. There were roses growing up a trellis against the wall but they weren't the same colour as the roses she used to put on Dad's grave.

"I liked those flowers you used to put on it because they were so different to mine. You didn't mind me throwing them away when they died, did you?"

247

Dad had moved to the side of the sofa. He was pulling at my shoulder. I lifted my hand in an effort to stop him.

"I like things to be tidy, you see. Probably too tidy. It makes me feel safe."

I looked around her kitchen which was cluttered in an arty sort of way.

"But this is nice, cosy. I wanted to get in touch with you to ask you things about Dad, to ask you to tend the grave, but Mum said you'd moved and she'd lost your address. Why did she say that?"

"A misunderstanding perhaps. I did think about moving." It wasn't a proper reply, not one that explained everything.

"But you didn't."

"No. Do you think we ought to ring your mother and let her know that you're here?"

"She'll be fine. She thinks I'm with my friend Abi."

"Do you want to stop for lunch then? It's just a sandwich and some salad."

"I don't want to be any trouble."

"You're not. I'm in the middle of doing a painting for someone. I paint animals. But this is proving a bit difficult. I like to capture the character and I can't quite get it so a break will do me good."

"Can I see it?"

"Of course."

I suddenly had a horrible thought.

"Do you have any animals?"

"No," she said, heading for the stairs. "I used to have a big ginger cat but he died a couple of years ago. He was too special to replace."

I heaved a sigh of relief. That was one less thing to worry about.

Penny's work room was on the first floor at the front of the house. It was beautiful and light with two tall windows looking out on to identical houses opposite. At one end was a Victorian fireplace with tiles down either side featuring little blue birds. It was really pretty. Her work table was next to the window and on it was a half-finished watercolour of a horse.

"It's beautiful," I said. "You're really clever."

"Thank you," she replied. "Do you draw or paint?"

"No, I'm no good at it."

"You should be. Your mother's a very talented designer and your father could draw too."

"Could he? I didn't know that."

I ran my finger over her pot of brushes, breathed in the smell of paint, gazed at the pinboard covered with photographs and quotes and little bits torn from magazines.

"Did he come here, to this house?"

She pressed her lips together. "Yes."

"Were you close?"

"Like brother and sister, at one time."

"What happened?"

She sat down suddenly and gazed out of the window. "People change, Laura. They drift apart."

He was there, standing in the corner, very, very still. If he'd had any breath to hold he'd have been blue with the effort.

"Did *you* change," I paused, "or was it Dad?"

"Would you like to see some photographs of when we were young?" she asked, totally ignoring my question.

"Yes please," I replied.

She put her arm around my shoulder. "Then let's

get some lunch and we'll do that."

While Penny made us cheese and tomato sandwiches with some brown bread she'd baked that morning, she sent me outside to pick some rocket from a window box fixed underneath the kitchen window. Dad followed me into the little backyard.

"Laura, what on earth are we doing here?"

The phone went and Penny answered it.

"Won't be a minute," she called to me, wandering down the hall towards the front room.

"I had to bring you here and I knew you wouldn't come on your own."

"So you never were planning to meet up with your friends?"

"No."

"But why did you have to bring me so far away?" he asked, looking totally distraught.

"Because Gran is calling in the vicar to get rid of you. He's part of the Diocesan Deliverance Team and they go to houses to deal with spirits who are making a nuisance of themselves. That's why I had to get you out of the house, to somewhere you'd be completely safe. I thought if I found Penny, if I brought you here, you could stay until all the fuss dies down."

He raked his hands through his hair. "But here, Laura. Why here?"

"Because I thought you'd be happy here. But you're not and I don't understand why. She's really nice. Even if I told her about you I don't think she'd mind. I don't think she'd say I was completely crackers."

"But you're not going to tell her about me, are you?"

"No, not unless I have to."

I stared at him.

"You've got to promise me that you'll stay here, Dad."

"And if I promise, you'll go now? This minute?"

I started snipping at the rocket.

"Well I can't go straight away. That would look rude."

"All right then. But immediately after lunch – you'll go then?"

"Why, what's the hurry?"

"I don't want to have to leave you but if we have

got to part we'd better not drag it out."

"That's a bit melodramatic, isn't it?" I half laughed. "I mean, it's not as if we'll never see each other again. It's only for a little while, maybe just a few days or a couple of weeks. Then you can come back, once Gran is convinced that you've gone." I checked my watch. "I suppose I could send Abi a text and see if she's free for an hour or two."

"I thought you'd lost your phone."

"Yes, so did I. I found it on the train. It was in my rucksack all the time. Silly me!"

He just raised his eyebrows. He may not have been around for years but he wasn't fooled at all.

We sat outside in Penny's tiny garden to eat our lunch and she leafed through an album of photos showing her and Dad as they were growing up. She told me all sorts of things that I never knew, like how she and Dad wanted to build a tunnel to each other's houses. Dad started his in the back garden and when his father found out he was really cross. Apparently Dad's father was very strict.

"I don't think they quite knew how to deal with your father," Penny said. "He was quite a naughty little boy, always getting up to mischief. I'm the youngest of three sisters and I was a bit of a tomboy when I was small. Your father and I were only six months apart in age. I thought he was such fun." She put a bowl of cherries in the centre of the table and told me about her time at art college and how hard it had been when she first started out.

"Do you know what you want to do when you leave school?" she asked me.

I shook my head. "I work hard but I'm not clever. I'm about in the middle of the class and don't have a particular talent for anything so I'm not sure what I'll end up doing. Something boring probably."

"Don't say that!" She sounded genuinely upset. "I'm sure you've got lots of talents. Maybe you just haven't tapped in to them yet. There's plenty of time. Some people take ages to find their direction in life."

I wanted to stay and talk to her for longer but Dad was pointing at my watch.

"I'd better be going. Can I help you to clear up first?"

"No, definitely not. There's hardly anything to do."

I asked to use the bathroom and she directed me

upstairs. The door to her bedroom was slightly ajar. I don't know why I pushed it open and crept in. Next to the double bed was a photograph of a small child sitting in a flowerbed, holding a ginger kitten. She had curly brown hair and a heart-shaped face. I wondered if she was Penny's daughter because there was a definite family resemblance. When I came out of the bathroom Dad was standing on the landing and the bedroom door had been closed.

"You will be okay here, won't you?" I asked.

"Of course."

"I'll miss you."

"I'll miss you too," he said and his eyes looked all teary. "But it won't be for long, will it?"

"No."

"Promise?"

I smiled. "Yes, Dad. I promise."

"I've had the best time, Laura, these last few weeks. Getting to know you properly has been…" his voice was all croaky, "… amazing."

"It's been the same for me too, you know. And it's not goodbye for ever. It's just a short break."

He nodded. "You will take care of yourself?"

255

"Of course. You too."

"Laura," Penny's voice called up the stairs. "Is everything all right up there?"

"Fine," I said as I held out my arms to Dad and he held his back to me. Our fingers almost touched. I could feel a charge of electricity between us. A warmth spread through my whole body.

"Next best thing to a hug," he said.

"Yes," I whispered. "Thank you."

Downstairs in the hall Penny put her hands on both of my shoulders.

"I don't know exactly why you came, Laura, but I hope that I've answered some of your questions. Will you come and see me again?"

"Yes, I'd like that."

"Me too."

She bit her lip. "Send my love to your mother."

"I will."

"Are you going to see your friend now?"

I nodded although Abi hadn't replied to my text.

"And you'll take care travelling home?"

I nodded again.

Dad was standing next to her. I waved.

"See you soon," I said.

"I hope so," she replied but of course I wasn't really talking to her. I was talking to Dad.

He waved back and blew me a kiss. I smiled and closed the gate behind me. Mission accomplished.

Secrets

Abi still hadn't answered my text so I decided to go home. Not back to Derbyshire, which still didn't feel like home, but to my old house, my real home.

I stood on the opposite side of the road just staring at it for a couple of minutes. There were net curtains up at all of the windows and new blue pots crammed with African marigolds outside the front door. It didn't look at all like my house any more. Suddenly I wished that I really had arranged to see my old friends. Maybe they would stop me feeling so weird and displaced, as if I didn't really belong anywhere.

I couldn't stand on the pavement for ever so I began to walk towards the shops. I picked up some flowers from the florist two streets away and headed for the cemetery. Penny hadn't actually said whether she'd been to the grave so I thought I'd go and check.

Sure enough there was a little posy of roses and

white phlox but they'd obviously been there for some time and the petals were turning brown and falling off. I cleared them away, replaced them with my yellow daisies and sat on the bench for a while.

It was strange. There was no point in talking to Dad because I was pretty sure that he wasn't around. I'd half expected him to follow me when I left Penny's house but I had the feeling that he'd actually stayed put. I must have been really tired because my mind just went blank. That doesn't happen very often. I've usually got so many thoughts whizzing around inside my head that it can be exhausting. It was nice just to switch off. In fact I think that I almost dropped off to sleep. I jerked myself awake and blinked several times before checking my watch. It was almost five o'clock. Suddenly I didn't want to be here any more. I wanted to be back at the farm with Mum bustling around in the kitchen and the *clickety-clack* of Gran's knitting needles as she settled down to watch some quiz programme.

As I shrugged the rucksack onto my back a woman walked down the path towards me. It was the woman who had walked straight past me that day several weeks ago and put her flowers on an untended grave. I have no idea why but, before she noticed me, I slid off the bench and melted back into the shadow of the tree. The branches swept low and were full of leaves so I was partly hidden. I watched as the woman stopped by Dad's grave and looked at my fresh flowers. Then she looked towards me, straight through the lattice of leaves. I stared back, unsure what to do. A girl stepped forwards. She was holding a small bunch of pink and white flowers and must have been walking directly behind the woman so I hadn't spotted her before. I couldn't believe what I was seeing. She was younger than me, maybe about ten, and she was slimmer than I was at that age and maybe a little bit taller. But apart from that it was like looking at a younger version of myself. She was also definitely the girl from the photograph in Penny's bedroom.

"What is it?" she asked, following the woman's gaze.

I stepped forwards into the sunlight.

The woman put a hand on the girl's arm. "We

ought to go," she murmured.

"No!" the girl said, shaking her mother away and taking a tentative step towards me.

I had this enormous lump in my throat and I had no idea why. It felt like the size of an orange. Surely it must be grotesquely visible. The girl's face was serious but slightly inquisitive.

"Hello," she said.

I licked my lips. She waited, hands clenching the posy a little bit tighter. A petal dropped from one of the roses and landed on the back of her hand like a velvety pink teardrop. She didn't seem to notice.

"Hello," I replied.

The woman stood helplessly behind the girl. I could tell that she wanted them both to be spirited away, to be anywhere else except here.

"Are you Laura?" the girl asked.

Someone else who knew my name.

"Yes."

She smiled then, a beautiful, radiant smile. "I'm Daisy."

She said it as if I should know who she was. I must have shaken my head slightly, looked confused, because she glanced briefly behind her, as if looking for permission of some kind. The woman's eyes narrowed, *her* head definitely shook. The girl turned back towards me and hesitated.

"Are you Penny's daughter?" I asked.

Daisy's smile vanished in an instant. She looked upset.

"No," she said. "This is my mum."

I stared at the woman. "I don't understand."

She ignored me, took hold of her daughter's arm. The rose petal fluttered to the ground where it lay between us.

"Daisy, we really ought to be going."

The girl stood her ground. "I haven't put my flowers on Daddy's grave yet," she protested.

The woman closed her eyes as Daisy walked purposefully forwards, retrieved the jam jar from behind the headstone and placed her posy in it.

Inside my head everything was swimming. I watched in disbelief as she settled the jar full of flowers next to my yellow daisies. I felt cold and clammy and my eyes couldn't focus properly. There was this rushing in my ears.

"Laura, Laura, are you all right?"

The woman's voice came from very far away, as if she were at the end of a long tunnel. I was aware of her grabbing my arm and leading me back to the bench, easing me down, gently pressing my head towards my knees.

"Better?" she asked, after a couple of minutes. "I'm sorry. You've had a bit of a shock."

I nodded. That was the understatement of the year.

"There must be some mistake," I whispered. "I don't understand."

Daisy stood in front of me, her face full of concern. "It isn't a mistake, is it, Mummy?" she asked the woman. "Laura is my sister, isn't she?"

How do you describe a moment like that? It was like my world caving in and opening up all at the same time. It was disbelief and recognition, excitement and blame. It was a huge tangle of questions tying me up in knots. It was beyond belief, and yet as I looked at her standing in front of me, unsure whether I'd ever be able to remember how to activate the right facial muscles and smile again, I knew that it was true.

"How?" I asked.

What a stupid question. There was obviously only one explanation but before the woman got the time to answer her mobile phone rang. She ignored it. It rang again.

"You'd better answer that," I murmured. "It could be important."

In truth I wanted some space, some time to think, or not think. I just wanted time. I sat, only half listening while she spoke. I remembered learning about the five stages of grief – denial, anger, bargaining, depression and acceptance. In the space of about thirty seconds my mind turbo-charged through the first four but when it got to acceptance it felt like running into a brick wall. NEVER. This could *not* be true and yet looking at Daisy I knew it was. Suddenly my whole body was so angry that I barely remember springing from the seat.

"No," the woman was saying, "it's too late. She's here. I'm sorry. I didn't expect…"

I lunged for the phone, wrenched it from her grasp and pressed it against my ear.

"Who is this?" I bellowed.

There was a gaping silence. Sometime, someone was going to feel the need to fill it and it wasn't going to be me.

"It's me."

The voice was soft and quiet, barely audible through the noise of a plane passing overhead. "It's me, Penny. I'm so sorry you had to find out like this."

"Penny," I shouted. "You knew? It's true?"

"I can't talk about this over the phone. Why don't you all come back here and have a cup of tea?"

"That photo by your bed. I saw it and thought it looked like me. I thought it was *your* daughter."

"Daisy is my god-daughter."

Daisy. Dad's other daughter. She was watching me, frightened now, since I grabbed the phone like a person possessed. She looked like a little cornered mouse watching a cat, waiting for it to make its next move. I thrust the phone back at the woman and bent forwards, put my head in my hands. I had a half-sister. For all of these years I had a sister and no one had told me.

Half an hour later I was, once more, pushing open the gate to Penny's front garden. She'd obviously been looking out for us because the door opened before we'd even reached the porch.

We hadn't spoken on the way over. The woman, whose name was Amanda, had driven us in her car. I sat in the back and tried to ignore the way her eyes kept checking up on me in the rear-view mirror. Daisy was upset now too. She thought that she shouldn't have said anything, that everyone would be cross with her. I think she was crying a little but I was feeling too detached to care. That wasn't right, was it? If she was really my sister then I would feel something, wouldn't I? I'd want to comfort her. But I didn't. So perhaps it was all some terrible mistake after all. Except that of course I knew it wasn't.

"Laura."

Penny reached out to touch my arm but I brushed her away. She had no right to touch me, to pretend to be all caring and concerned. I wanted to rush around to look for Dad but I didn't need to. He sloped into the hall and from the look on his face he obviously wanted to be anywhere else than here, maybe even back with Gran and Reverend Tim. I couldn't even bear to look him in the eye.

"Tea," Penny said, leading us into the sitting room. "I've made tea. Do you drink tea, Laura?"

I nodded and she put a bone china cup and saucer in my hands. Why hadn't she used mugs? Was it so that I had to concentrate more in order not to spill the hot, sweet liquid onto her pale-blue silk cushions? I put the tea on the table in front of me.

"Laura, I can explain," Dad whispered in my ear. I lifted my hand and brushed him away.

"How did you know my name?" I asked Daisy.

The woman, Amanda, spoke. She was sitting on the edge of the chair, her hand resting lightly on Daisy's shoulder.

"Daisy has always known about you," she said. "I've told her ever since she was a baby that she had a sister and her name was Laura. I'd always hoped that one day you two would meet but not quite like this."

"I don't understand what Penny's got to do with this," I said.

"Amanda is a friend," Penny explained. "She and your father met at a party of mine. Daisy was only two weeks old when he died. Your mother had her family to rally around. Amanda didn't have anyone. I didn't approve of what she and your father had done but I tried to be supportive."

"Did my mum know about you?" I asked Amanda.

"Yes."

Still I wouldn't, couldn't, look at Dad.

"Was he going to leave us, for you?"

Over by the window Dad shook his head furiously. I shifted on my seat so that he was out of my line of vision.

"Maybe," Amanda replied. "I can't pretend that I didn't want him to."

I was shaking now. I couldn't get my head around this. I wanted to get away, to be back in my room at the farm, somewhere quiet and peaceful where I could lie down and fall into a deep sleep. Then, maybe when I woke up, I would find out that it had all been a horrible dream. I stood up. My tea rippled as I placed the cup and saucer on the uneven table top.

"I've got a train to catch."

"Laura, you're upset," Penny said. "You can't go yet."

"You can't stop me."

Daisy's face was so white. She looked as if she was about to burst into tears. I was an expert on when people were about to cry. I'd had enough experience myself.

"I'm sorry," I said to her. "None of this is your fault."

She blinked and sure enough a couple of tears lodged on her upper cheek. "I thought you'd be happy," she sniffed.

It was one of those moments that can define your future, define someone else's too. I knew instinctively that the answer I gave would have an impact on both of our lives, for better or for worse. Be a grown-up, Laura, I said to myself. Show Daisy that you're the sort of person she'd be proud to call her sister. I didn't want to be sensible and mature and reasonable though. I wanted to rage and stamp about and shout. But I looked at Daisy with her red-rimmed eyes and quivering bottom lip and somehow I got a grip on myself.

"I'm sorry," I said again. For goodness' sake, why was *I* the one who kept apologising? "It's just been such a shock, that's all. I had no idea, none at all. No one warned me."

I did look at Dad then, shot him a look as full of disappointment and venom as I could muster.

There was this uncomfortable silence in the room. No one knew what to say to me and my head was clogged with angry, resentful thoughts that were kicking my insides to pieces. I wanted to be better than those thoughts so I scrabbled in my rucksack and pulled out a piece of paper and a pencil.

"Here's my mobile number. You can text me if you like."

I wasn't even sure whether I wanted her to but just saying the words helped. I did feel a tiny bit better about myself. I shoved the pad back in my rucksack and made for the door. Dad was right by my side.

"Can I come with you to the station?" Penny asked. "Make sure that you get on the train safely?"

"I'd rather you didn't."

I didn't mean to sound so rude but the last thing I wanted was her fussing around me, trying to make polite conversation, trying to justify her actions.

"Will you send me a text when you get back then?" She pushed a business card into my hand. "Please?"

I nodded, partly because I'd have agreed to anything just to get out of there, just for them all to leave me alone and stop staring at me as if I were some newly discovered prize specimen. As I left Dad was standing on the doorstep, mouthing the word "Sorry," so many times that I lost count. And that's where I thought he'd stayed but, as I turned the corner at the bottom of the street, he materialised beside me.

"What are *you* doing here?" I groaned.

"I want to explain. I really didn't want you to find out like this."

"What is there to explain? You were having an affair. You had another child. You might have been about to leave Mum and me. I'm probably not your favourite daughter after all. I don't expect

271

you wanted me to find out at all. End of."

"Laura, it's not like that."

"I bet! Leave me alone, Dad, will you? Go and spend some time with your other daughter while I sort my life out."

And I marched off, leaving him standing looking lonely and sad by a crossroads sign. Apt or what?

EXPLAINING

Mum was waiting on the platform at Derby station. I spotted her before I'd even got off the train and to be honest I was tempted to duck down and carry on to Sheffield, except I didn't know anyone there and then what would I do? I could tell from her strained expression that Penny had been in touch and told her everything. I got off the train and walked straight past, avoiding eye contact. She hurried to catch up with me and I shifted my bag from one shoulder to the other so that it formed a buffer between us.

"Are you all right?" she asked quietly, the words almost whisked away in the slamming of doors and clatter of heels on asphalt. "I know what happened and I'm sorry."

It's funny how that word 'sorry' can make you so angry when it's meant to do the opposite. I kept silent, kept walking fast so she had to make an effort to keep up with me.

I inserted my ticket into the slot at the barrier while an official waved Mum through. We headed out towards the car.

"I've been so worried about you," she gasped. "You didn't answer your mobile."

"That's because I didn't want to talk to anybody. Can't think why, can you?"

"I did what I thought was best, Laura. That's why I didn't tell you."

I stopped. In the middle of the spot where the taxis turned.

"So were you ever going to tell me? Or was it something you thought I didn't need to know? After all, it's not particularly important, is it?"

A taxi hooted at me. I couldn't care less. Mum reached for my arm. I flinched myself out of her reach.

"I have a half-sister. You had no right to keep that from me."

She looked as if she was about to burst into tears. "You don't understand…"

"No, I don't."

"And neither do I," called a cab driver, "and I don't particularly want to, so can you carry on this conversation somewhere else, ladies?"

I glared at him.

"Laura," Mum begged, "you can't stand here. You're getting in the way."

Reluctantly I stepped to the side and she shepherded me towards the car.

"So," I said, as soon as she settled behind the steering wheel, before she'd had the chance to start the engine, "can you explain why everyone else knew and I didn't? Even Liberty knew that the fairy tale you'd concocted wasn't true. Even my own cousin knew more about my life than I did."

"Not everyone knew," Mum said weakly, twizzling her wedding ring.

"All those years you lied about who was putting flowers on the grave and you knew."

She half turned towards me. "Yes, I knew."

"Did you know that Dad was having an affair before he died?"

"Yes, I knew that too. Eventually. They met at Penny's house. It was a Christmas party and

 275

everyone had had a bit too much to drink. I remember your father spent a lot of time talking to this very attractive woman in a green silk dress. We rowed about it when we got home. He said I was being silly and jealous and that she was new to the area and didn't know many people. He said he was just being friendly."

She gulped as if struggling for air.

"Then he started to say he was working late or meeting someone for a drink and I believed him."

She was crying now.

"How stupid can you get?"

She looked at me, tears streaming down her face, mascara smudging in the hollows under her eyes.

"In the end I confronted him. He lied at first but then he confessed. He said he was going to finish it and I believed him. He could be so charming, so loving. I wanted to trust him."

She half smiled.

"I never thought he'd leave us, and then on the day of the funeral *she* turned up. Holding a baby. She sat at the back in the church, near the door, behind a pillar, but I'd spotted her. Everyone had.

A month-old baby at a funeral does tend to attract attention. Can you imagine how humiliating, how shocking that was for me, Laura?"

I had such a vivid picture of it all in my head that, yes, I could imagine.

"I'm really, really sorry. I know that I should have told you but I found it so difficult to accept and very quickly you started to build your father up into this fantastic person, this hero, the sort of devoted daddy every little girl longs for. I couldn't shatter that image."

I tried to take in all that she had said, tried to understand it from Mum's point of view.

"But I have a sister," I repeated, more calmly now. "Have you any idea how much I longed for that?"

She wiped her eyes, looked at me confusedly. "I thought you were happy."

I shook my head. "It's not about being happy or unhappy." I hesitated, struggling for an explanation. People say that you can't miss what you've never had. That's not true. I'd never had a brother or a sister but I'd still missed the ones I might have had, the ones I wanted. I'd never liked the fact that it was just me. People make assumptions about only children and they're usually not very complimentary.

"I'd rather not have been alone," I said. "I'd have liked someone to play with, to fight with, to talk to, to share my growing up."

"You've had Liberty."

"It's not the same."

How could I explain that now I had met Daisy, seen how her brown hair was blond at the edges the same as mine, the way her eyebrows had that slight kink the same as mine, the way her voice sounded similar in pitch to mine, it had opened up a huge chasm inside of me, a sense of loss.

"Sisters don't always get on, you know."

I was silent for a moment. "I just wish that we'd had the chance to not get on," I said. "You never let me find that out and we only lived forty-five minutes apart. Would you ever have told me?"

"Of course."

"When?"

"When the time was right."

"And when would that have been?"

"I don't know." She covered her eyes with her hands.

"Now I know why Gran never liked Dad," I said. "That's why she was so keen for you to make a fresh start. I suppose *she* insisted that I mustn't be told any of this."

Mum moved her hands away and looked at me.

"No," she said, "you're wrong. Your gran was very much in favour of telling you, right from the start."

I leaned my head against the coolness of the window and looked at my reflection in the glass. I was tired and confused. I wanted to go home. I wanted to be with someone who understood me and, weird as it seemed, that person was Gran.

She was waiting in the kitchen when we got back. The kettle was on and she was already wearing her dressing gown. Her hair was down but held back on one side with a sparkly pink clip. As I walked in she leaned back against the range and opened her arms. I didn't hesitate. I walked straight into them. She smelled of lemon shower gel, and the dressing gown was soft against my cheek. I wanted to cry but I was too tired, too washed out. She didn't speak, just stroked my hair with one hand and held me tightly with the other. I wanted to stay like that for ever, with my eyes closed and my mind blank.

"A nice toasted teacake," Gran said at last. "That's what you need, and a hot drink, followed by a good night's sleep."

I didn't argue although to sleep after the day I'd had seemed hopelessly optimistic. But by the time I got into bed my eyelids were so heavy they felt as if they were coated with concrete. Mum knocked tentatively on my door. I'd barely spoken to her since we'd got back.

"Are you feeling better?"

What a dumb question. Of course I wasn't feeling better. My whole world had suddenly been turned on its head. People I thought I could trust had turned out to be lying to me, and Gran, whom I'd never liked, never trusted, was suddenly the only person in the world who seemed worth bothering with.

"Yeah, I'm fine," I replied, hoping my sleepiness

hadn't curbed the sarcastic edge too much.

"Liz," I heard Gran's voice whispering up from the bottom of the stairs. "Leave her alone. Let her sleep."

But Mum wouldn't leave me alone. She came in and stood by my bed for a while, watching me while I willed her to go away. Finally she left and I listened with relief as she made her way downstairs. I snuggled deeper under my duvet, thinking that my room felt cold because I was so exhausted. Stupid of me not to realise the real reason.

"Laura, are you awake?"

I groaned, opened one eye. Dad was bending over me, hands clasped together in front of his chest. "When your world's been blown apart you're hardly likely to fall into a blissful sleep, are you?" I muttered.

He flinched. I opened the other eye.

"What are you doing here? You're meant to be staying put in London, remember?"

Secretly, I was pleased he was there, that he hadn't just left me to stew, but there was no way

 281

I was going to tell him that.

"I couldn't just leave you at the end of the road. You weren't thinking clearly. I was worried about you. There are always things to worry about when you're a parent – drugs, drink, sex, exam stress…"

"And secret families," I added dryly.

He straightened up, then sank onto the bed. I could see the bright pink flower pattern from my duvet through his jeans.

"I'm so, so sorry. I didn't mean you to find out like that. I knew that I ought to tell you about Daisy myself but…"

I stared at him, trying to fathom what he was thinking, what he was feeling.

"But you bottled it, because really you didn't mean me to find out at all?"

"I didn't want to hurt you. I've never ever wanted to hurt you."

I made a choking noise. "You didn't think about that when you were in bed with Amanda, did you?"

He winced. "Don't be crude, Laura. It doesn't become you."

I shook my head. "Well, I'm so sorry but I'm not

282

the perfect, forgiving daughter you think that I am. You've cheated me, Dad. You've let me down."

I wished I could cry. Get all of that anger out. Instead it was burning inside of me, making my every muscle feel as if it had set solid.

"Do you think I don't know that? I've let everyone down. I want to try and explain, if you'll let me."

He reached out, as if to touch my hair, my cheek. If I hadn't instinctively moved away he might have actually made contact with me. Instead I just felt a tingle of energy and something like a crescent of disappointment falling away with the curve of his hand.

"I'm not perfect, Laura. Far from it, but I'm trying to be a better father. When you're fourteen you think that adulthood is some defined moment, as if when you reach twenty or twenty-five then you'll be a grown-up, as if you've stepped over a line in the sand. You think that you'll feel differently, be more confident maybe, more able to cope with what life throws at you. You think that you'll have all of the answers. It's not like that. Growing up is something that takes a lifetime, whether you live to thirty-one like me or seventy-four like Grandad. Most people do their growing up in stages and, looking back, I was probably a bit behind everyone else of my age. I was certainly behind your mother, even though she's younger than me. When you were born I wasn't ready to give up my other life, the one where I could just go out and have fun without worrying about other responsibilities. I know it sounds weak and pathetic but, although I loved you more than you will ever know, I found it difficult to settle down to family life. Your mum seemed to take to it much more naturally and that made me feel so inadequate. She coped so well with you that it seemed that I wasn't really needed."

So he was blaming Mum now for his weakness. I put my hands over my ears.

"Stop it! I don't want to hear any more excuses. You blew it, Dad. You blew it then and you've blown it now. Go back to where you came from." I held up my hand. "I know you've said that you can't, but to be honest I don't believe you. Why should I believe anything you say any more? You've lied about the past so there's no reason why you wouldn't lie about your return journey as well, is there?"

He looked genuinely shocked. "Is that really what you want?"

You know when you say things that you don't really mean but you just can't help yourself? This was one of those times.

"Yes, it is."

How can three such tiny words have such power? How can they convey something so massive, that it can change your entire future? He was quiet for a moment as if taking it in.

"Whatever I did in the past, Laura, it didn't mean I stopped loving you. You are my firstborn. I remember the very first time I held you in my arms and looked down into your beautiful blue eyes. I had never felt anything like that rush of love. I may have made mistakes but that love for you never went away. You are my special girl. You are the best thing that ever happened to me."

I bit my lip, wished he'd stop trying to make everything better. It couldn't, wouldn't, work.

"I love you, Laura. You can think what you like.

285

You can send me away, but wherever I am, wherever you are, nothing you say or do will ever change that."

And before I had the chance to reply he faded away.

I lay there for ages, wide awake, watching the moonbeams streaking across the bottom of my bed, listening to the grandfather clock in the hall chiming on the half hour. Part of me wished that Dad had never come back, that I could have carried on living my life believing that he was a hero. But you can't reverse time. You have to deal with what you've been given and you have to make the best of it. In reality I wouldn't have swapped those weeks with Dad, finding out about him and about myself.

"Dad?" I called into the semi-darkness. "Are you there?"

A creaking floorboard on the landing, the *tick-tock* of the clock, but no reply.

I sat up again.

"You won't go without saying goodbye, will you, Dad?"

Still no reply.

CRISIS

I woke with a start. Sat up. Looked at the corner of the room. The chair was empty. What had I done? I didn't really want him to go. I wanted to have him with me for ever and ever. How could he not know that?

As I slouched down the stairs in my dressing gown the whole house felt churned up with emotion. Guilt, anger, grief. They were all swirling around, buzzing in and out of the nooks and crannies like those mortar bees that eat away at houses. I just knew that I would never forgive myself for sending him away like that. But when I stepped into the kitchen Dad was standing by the window, reading the paper over Gran's shoulder. He lifted his hand in a little wave and sent me a smile. It was a smile full of regret and nervousness. 'I'm still here,' the smile said, 'is that okay?'

I smiled back, gave a small nod. I wanted to rush over and hug him, to feel his arms wrapping around me and hear him telling me that everything was okay. Fathers and daughters fell out. Sometimes they fell out big time like my friend Abi and her dad but you could always make up, even after years and years. It just took someone to be brave, to make the first move, for someone to stay put when you told them to go. Gran looked up from the article she was reading, gazed at my dressing gown and put the paper down on the table.

"How are you feeling this morning?" she asked, looking over the top of her glasses.

I reached for the cereal. "Fine. Thanks."

"You don't look fine."

"Thanks."

Mum bustled into the kitchen with a list in one hand and a basket in the other.

"I'm going to the farmers' market," Mum said to me. "I thought you might like to come. It'll do you good to get out of the house, to take your mind off things. You'll have to hurry up and get dressed though. I've got a lot to do."

I wasn't ready for another intense conversation with Mum and once she had me in the car there would be no getting away from it.

"I'll stay here with Gran."

"She'll be all right left for a while. Won't you, Mother? You've been moving a bit better recently."

Gran shifted in her chair and winced. She was making a really good job of looking pathetic.

"Yes, I have, but do you know, Liz, I feel a bit weak today. It must be all the upset. It's not good for you when you get older. If Laura could stay with me I'd feel much happier."

Mum looked annoyed. I stared down at my toast.

"All right then," she slightly snapped, "but we'll have a proper talk when I get back, Laura. You can't avoid me for ever." She turned to Gran. "And don't think I haven't cottoned on to what you're up to. I'm surprised at you, Mother! You're the one who's been on at me all these years to tell Laura the truth and now I want to explain things to her properly you're putting obstacles in my way."

Before Gran had the time to reply, Mum had

stormed out of the room.

"Why don't you go with her?" I mouthed to Dad, picking up the box of cereal and heading for the pantry.

He followed me, blowing the door almost closed so that Gran couldn't hear me whispering.

"I hoped we could spend some time together today," he said.

"Maybe later," I said. He looked anguished. "I just need a bit of space, that's all. I'm glad you're still here."

He leaned very close. I was sure I could feel breath coming from his mouth as he spoke. "I wouldn't have left you, Laura, even if I could. I'm not going to leave you again. We can sort this out. I know we can. We can get back to where we were before."

I nodded. "Maybe. You just need to give me time."

"Then I'll go to the farmers' market this morning," he said. "I'll do whatever you want me to do. I want to make it up to you, Laura. To show you how sorry I am."

"Yes," I said. "I know you do."

After Mum and Dad had gone I went into the garden and sat on the swing seat. I closed my eyes and rocked myself gently as I thought about my parents and Amanda and Daisy. I'd been there for about ten minutes when Gran appeared, treading carefully over the cobbles. I moved across and she sank down next to me.

"So," she said, watching one of the swallows swoop in and out of its nest under the eaves, "is he still here?"

"Who?"

Then she turned and looked me straight in the eyes. "Don't play games with me, Laura. You know exactly who I mean. Your father."

I was too tired to lie. "Yes... and no."

She raised an eyebrow.

"I tried to take him to London. That's why I went, to get rid of him for a while. I heard you on the phone to the vicar and..." My voice petered away. "I couldn't let that happen. I couldn't let you exterminate him."

"You *tried* to take him to London. I take it you didn't succeed?"

"Yes, I did actually. It wasn't easy but in the end he came with me and I told him to stay there, with Penny."

"But let me guess," Gran continued, "he didn't do as he was told."

I shook my head. "I thought he had and then he appeared in my room last night."

"So where is he now?" Gran asked, scanning the garden. "Perched in a tree, messing up my potting shed, lying on the grass in front of us?"

"He's gone with Mum to the farmers' market. I told him I needed some space."

Gran looked suddenly alarmed.

"So he's in the car with her?"

"Yes."

I don't know why but a sudden chill went through my heart, like when you've had ice cream that's too cold.

"Why?" I asked. "Shouldn't he be?"

She didn't answer, just started picking at a bit of loose cotton on her skirt.

"Gran, what is it? What's the matter?"

"Nothing."

She was lying, trying to protect me from something.

"Gran, tell me what's wrong."

She smoothed the folds of her skirt and traced

a finger around the pattern. "I know that you think you probably know everything, Laura," she blurted out, "but when your father died in that accident there wasn't anyone else involved." The words came so fast they almost merged into one another.

The cold feeling was like a shard of ice now. Maybe I was about to have a heart attack like Grandad. "I don't know what you mean. Mum said that he swerved to avoid a car that was pulling out of another lane on the motorway."

"No," Gran said softly. "That's not true. He may have swerved to avoid something, a fox or a rabbit maybe, but there wasn't another car nearby. He was going too fast, Laura, and he turned the car over and crashed into the central barrier. It's as simple as that."

Now my throat was all constricted.

"He was on the way back from seeing *her*, the other woman," Gran continued, more slowly now, more measured. "She'd just had the child and I suppose he was running late."

"He'd promised me a bedtime story," I whispered. "It was my fault he was rushing."

293

Gran put her hand on my knee. "NO!" It came out so forcefully that I jumped. "Don't say that, Laura. Don't think that. It's not true. Your father always drove too fast. To be honest, it was an accident waiting to happen."

I tried to take all of this in and then I thought of Mum. I put my hand over Gran's. It was trembling slightly.

"It'll be all right, Gran. He's not driving this time. Mum is. Besides, he's not stupid and he's been in the car with her before, a couple of weeks ago. He won't do anything to hurt her."

She tried to smile. "I'm sure you're right, Laura. I'm sure he's changed."

"He has. When your tablets went missing he helped to find them."

She looked surprised. "Then I'm sure everything will be just fine and I'm just a silly old woman who's worrying us both for nothing."

But it wasn't fine. Mum had said that she'd be back at one o'clock, one-thirty at the latest. By ten to two, Gran and I should have been starving but we weren't. We were too worried to eat. I'd tried Mum's mobile five times but there was no reply.

"Contact your father," Gran said. "Doesn't he hear you when you call? Isn't that how he 'came over' in the first place?"

"Yes," I replied. "But he doesn't always respond."

"Try," she begged.

I cleared my throat and stood in the middle of the kitchen. "Dad," I called as loudly and clearly as I could. "Where are you? Are you with Mum? Can you let us know that everything's all right? We're really worried."

I stood, my head tilted back, eyes fixed towards the ceiling where a small jagged crack had broken through the wallpaper. Gran was very still. I think we were both holding our breath. Listening. Waiting. Hoping. But there was no sound apart from the hum of the fridge and the ticking of the clock and beyond that the deep, hollow space of silence.

"Dad, please!" I tried again. "If you can hear me, just let us know that you're both okay."

I shook my head. "It's no good. I'm sorry."

Gran covered her face with her hands briefly and then sat up ramrod straight. She was looking really pale so I opened a tin of soup.

"You know what Mum's like," I said. "She's probably met someone she used to go to school with and they're having a coffee somewhere."

"She'd have phoned to let us know," Gran said.

"Maybe there's a problem with her phone. Maybe she's broken down in a place without signal."

"It's ringing, isn't it?" Gran replied.

There was no answer to that. She was right. We managed a few mouthfuls of soup and a bit of bread but it tasted metallic and I was beginning to feel sick. I kept going to the front door and looking up and down the road to see if there was any sign of her, as if looking would suddenly make her appear. At quarter to three Gran announced she was going to ring Aunt Jane.

"Isn't she at some conference today?" I said, covering Gran's legs with a blanket, even though it wasn't particularly cold. "Why don't I go and find Uncle Pete? He'll know what to do."

"He's harvesting the top field. You know how he hates to be disturbed. The weather's set to change too. He needs to get it done."

I shrugged, beginning to feel desperate. Surely Mum was more important than a few grains of wheat but the way they'd given us the cold shoulder recently I didn't want to bet on it.

"What do you want me to do?" I asked. "Ring around the hospitals?" That was what they did in films, wasn't it?

She shook her head. "No, I'll do it."

But I could see she wasn't up to it. There was the sound of a car pulling into the drive at the side of the house and I ran to the window.

"Please let it be Mum," I prayed, but in my heart I knew that the engine didn't have quite the same note.

"Who is it, Laura?" Gran called. "Is it Liz?"

"No," I tried to shout back, although my voice felt weak. "It's the vicar."

"Oh my goodness," Gran said. "I'd completely forgotten that he'd said he was calling in to see me."

By the time I led Reverend Tim through to the sitting room and explained the situation, tears were streaming down my face. Ever since Dad's accident

297

I couldn't bear people being late. My mind just zoomed into overdrive and I suppose that I was overwrought from the previous day but I totally went to pieces. Sam had been sitting in the front seat of the car and that's where I'd wanted him to stay but his dad called him inside. He looked at me and sort of smiled. I know he was trying to be reassuring and I should have been grateful but I was too panic-stricken to appreciate anything except the sense of dread that had taken over every cell of my body. I wanted to be rational, to be in control, to tell myself that I was being silly. But when you've lost one parent you always feel as if you're on a precipice, as if the slightest tilt of the landscape could make your world slide towards catastrophe again. When I was little and having nightmares Mum used to reassure me. "Lightning doesn't strike in the same place twice," she had said.

And I had wanted to believe her. Then I read about a man on a golf course who'd actually been struck by lightning – twice. So I knew that bad things could happen to you more than once in your life. Reverend Tim draped an arm around my shoulders and pulled me closer to him. He flourished a pristine white handkerchief from his pocket and pressed it into my hand.

"I'm sure there's a perfectly reasonable explanation for this," he said and his voice was melodic, almost as if he was reading out a psalm, but it was calming too. "So, let's not panic and start imagining the worst."

He pressed his fingers gently into the top of my shoulder as I dried my eyes.

"Laura, I want you and Sam to go and make some tea while I ring around a few places. Can you manage to do that?"

I nodded. But to be honest I'd rather have done it on my own.

"It'll be okay," Sam said, as I spooned tea into the teapot and waited for the kettle to boil.

"You don't know that," I replied.

We stood in an awkward silence and I wished he'd go back to the sitting room. Maybe if I didn't talk to him he would.

"I wish you'd told me about your dad."

I rearranged the tea towels on the front of

the range. He obviously wasn't picking up on my subliminal messages.

"You'd have thought I was nuts."

"No, I wouldn't. My dad deals with that sort of thing all of the time."

"I didn't know that then."

He put the sugar bowl on the tray. "Is that why you gave Gloria back, because of your dad?"

"How did you know that?"

He shrugged. "You seemed so besotted with her. There must have been a good reason for you to suddenly turn up on my doorstep, a few minutes after setting off home, and thrusting the box into my arms without any explanation."

"Dad's allergic to cats."

"Couldn't he have just kept his distance?"

"He said it was him or the cat."

"Oh!" Sam said. "That's mean."

I wanted to defend Dad, to say that I understood why he had made me do it, but I couldn't because try as I might I didn't understand.

"I haven't seen you around," Sam said. "Have you been avoiding me?"

Why was the kettle taking so long to boil? Was it part of some conspiracy to add to my torture?

"No, of course not." Too emphatic, Laura. You've given yourself away there. "I saw you with Liberty." Why did I say that? Why didn't I just shut up and keep my stupid thoughts to myself?

"When?"

As if he didn't remember. How naive did he think I was?

"Last week. You were walking down the road together." Very close. I pressed my lips together and turned away, towards the kettle.

"I bumped into her, that's all."

Literally, by the looks of things.

"Laura!"

I hadn't heard him move. When he touched my shoulder, I jumped so high that I almost hit my head on the shelf fixed to the wall above the range.

"What?"

"I don't... you know... fancy her."

I didn't believe him but I played along. My brain was too scrambled to do anything else.

"Don't you?"

"No, she's not my type."

The kettle started to vibrate. A little puff of steam came from the spout. I watched it evaporate in front of me.

"She's too high maintenance *and* she wants to be the centre of attention all the time. I couldn't be doing with someone like that." He sounded genuine. "I am right, aren't I?"

I turned, almost smiled. "Yeah, she's fairly full on. It can get a bit much."

There was a shift in the atmosphere as if some tightness in the air had slackened a little.

"I'm surprised that you two are so close. You're so different."

I lifted the kettle off and poured water into the teapot. "You know what they say, blood is thicker than water."

Then I thought of Mum and what I would do if I lost her too and if I hadn't concentrated hard on making that tea, the tears would have flowed again.

DECISIONS

"We've found her," Gran said as I followed Sam back into the sitting room. He'd insisted on holding the tray.

"Where?" I gasped. "Is she okay?"

Gran nodded and I could see she was on the point of tears too. "There's been an accident but she's all right. They've taken her to hospital with mild concussion."

I sank down onto the nearest chair and dropped my head to my knees. They felt bony against my forehead. "Thank you, thank you, thank you," I mouthed towards the carpet.

"Laura." Reverend Tim put a hand on my shoulder. "Drink this."

I uncurled and took the mug of tea. "Can we go and see her?" I asked.

"When you've drunk your tea," he replied. "Then I'll take you."

We settled Gran in the front of the old Volvo and Sam put a small cushion at her back. Then he slid onto the rear seat next to me. There was a box of tissues between us. We didn't speak, just listened to Gran and Reverend Tim chatting away about people in the village and the history of the church. I wanted to ask about Gloria, about whether Sam had managed to find another home for her, but I didn't dare. I couldn't bear to hear that she was happily living with someone else.

Mum was in a long ward with old silver pipes running around the wall near to the ceiling. We'd had to put Gran in a wheelchair to get there because it was down corridors that twisted and turned and seemed to go on for ever. Sam and his dad weren't going to come in. They were going to wait outside in the car park but the wheelchair was so heavy and cumbersome, even before Gran got into it, that there was no way I'd have been able to push it all that way. Even Reverend Tim had trouble getting it to go in the right direction and ended up pulling

Gran backwards, so she was facing me, and I took her right hand in my left one. Sam was on the other side of me and as we walked he touched my wrist. At first I thought it was accidental and then I felt the tips of his fingers pressing persistently against mine. I didn't turn to look at him, just let that lovely comforting feeling spread through me. When I did cast him a sideways glance his eyes flickered towards me. He was blushing and smiled, hesitantly, as if he wasn't sure that he was doing the right thing, as if he thought that at any moment I might give him the brush-off. Instead I closed the gap between us so that my fingers could curl around his. Out of the corner of my eye I saw his shoulders relax.

Mum was lying in bed, looking really woozy. She had a vivid red mark and an egg-shaped lump on the side of her head from where she'd hit the side window when the car had gone off the road. Dad was pacing up and down beside the bed. I put my arms around Mum, kissing her gently on the forehead.

"Laura?" she slurred. "Is that you?"

"Yes, Mum, and Gran's here too."

"I need to get the supper," she continued, trying to lift herself up.

I pressed her back down. "No, you don't. You've got to stay here. You've had a bang on the head. You're confused."

"Confused," she repeated. "So confused."

Reverend Tim helped Gran towards the chair.

"Why are you all here?" Mum asked. "Are we having a party? A nice glass of wine would do me good." She lifted her hand to her head. "Or have I had too many glasses already?"

We all smiled at that.

"Mind you, with what I've been through I need a few bottles, not glasses." She half lifted herself up. "Where is that man?" She looked at the chair where Gran was now sitting. "He was there. Watching me. Pretending he cares. But he doesn't really."

Her eyes were wild and unfocused but she latched them onto Dad who was hovering by the flowery curtain that separated the bed from the one next door. I knew that for the first time since he'd arrived back in our lives she could see him.

"I don't want him here. Get rid of him. Tell him to go away. He won't listen to me."

"Laura," Gran said, "take him out of here, will you, dear?"

For the first time I looked at Dad properly. He looked awful, really drawn.

"Come with me," I said and it was such a relief to be able to speak out loud in front of people, not to have to pretend any more.

He looked taken aback and I thought for a moment that he was going to be difficult but I gave him one of my best glares. He didn't dare refuse after that.

We stood outside in the corridor and I waited for a couple of nurses to bustle past.

"She could see me, Laura. But she doesn't want me there."

"It's the shock, that's all," I replied. "Why did she see you?"

He leaned back against the wall. "I could say it's because of the concussion but that would be a lie. It's because I wanted her to know that I was here." He looked at me then. "And before you say anything, this is all my fault. Your gran's right, Laura. Leopards don't change their spots. I'm just as selfish now as I was all of those years ago. I wanted your mother to see me. I wanted to tell her I was sorry. Me, me, me. It was all about me."

I should have been angry with him but I couldn't because he looked completely broken. His molecules were dancing all over the place. I took him out to the stairwell where it was easier to talk.

"What happened? Did she see you while she was driving along?"

He pressed his hands to his eyes. "So, so stupid of me. I didn't mean to appear in the car like that. I was just thinking about it, when would be the best time, and then this pheasant ran out from the hedge and I didn't think she'd seen it. I leaned over to grab the wheel. It was instinctive. I knew how upset she'd be if the car ran it over. And she must have felt my presence or even seen me. I don't know but the car swerved and she lost control and we ended up in the ditch."

"Are you all right?"

He took his hands away then and opened his eyes.

"Were you hurt?"

He shook his head. "Not physically anyway. I can't be injured in that way any more. But your mother could have been killed."

"But she wasn't. She's going to be fine."

"You'd have been orphaned because of my stupidity."

"Dad! Listen to me. Mum is going to be fine."

"I'm not safe to be around," Dad said. "You have to keep away from me, Laura. I'm a walking disaster. I'm not to be trusted. Never was."

He stumbled down the steps.

"Dad, don't be so stupid. Come back."

But he wasn't listening. He got to the bottom of the stairs and melted away.

They wanted to keep Mum in hospital overnight just to keep an eye on her. I kissed her lightly on the cheek.

"See you tomorrow, Mum."

"You'll be all right, Laura," she murmured. "Your father will look after you."

I stroked her hand. "I know, Mum. He wants to

 309

look after you too."

Reverend Tim stopped off and picked up fish and chips on the way home. I wasn't hungry but he said we had to eat and keep our strength up. He and Sam rummaged around in the kitchen getting out plates and ketchup and slicing bread while Gran and I gave them directions. When it was time for them to leave, Sam's dad put his hands on my shoulders and looked straight into my face.

"Laura, if you want to talk about this situation, you know where I am."

I nodded.

"Any time," he added.

"Thanks," I whispered.

"Will you both be all right tonight?"

"Yes," Gran replied, struggling to her feet and coming to wrap an arm around my waist. "We'll be fine."

"If you want anything just pick up the phone."

Sam reached out and touched my hand. "See you tomorrow," he said.

"Yes – yes please." And I felt the tears welling up all over again.

I was making hot chocolate when Gran came back into the kitchen. She'd gone to get changed into her nightie and I was so absorbed in stirring the milk, watching the little bubbles break on the surface as it came to the boil, that I didn't even hear the tap of her stick on the tiled floor.

"Laura."

I jumped.

"Gran, you scared me. I was miles away."

"With your mum?"

"Yes."

"She'll be all right."

"I know."

"She's such a careful driver." Gran was leaning on her stick, watching me.

"Yes."

"Have you any idea what happened?"

I lifted the saucepan off the heat and poured the frothy, chocolatey milk into two mugs. I needed time to think. "It wasn't what you think. He wasn't trying to make her go faster."

I told her what Dad had told me.

"Accidents happen, don't they?" I said.

311

Her eyes were glinting black in the half-light.

I put one mug onto a tray with a couple of ginger biscuits and offered to carry it through to her room.

"Yes, they do," she replied. "But it can't be allowed to happen again, Laura. You know that, don't you?"

"Yes," I said, so quietly that I'm surprised she heard me. Then I went over and pressed my cheek to hers before going upstairs to bed.

I barely slept. I heard the clock in the hall strike midnight, then one, then two, then three o'clock.

Time seemed to have slowed down but I realised I didn't actually mind. For once, the slower time moved the better. Because when morning came I knew what I would have to do and it was going to be one of the most difficult things I had ever done in my entire life.

I had set my alarm on my phone for eight o'clock but I didn't need it. I was awake at half past seven and lay there, staring at the ceiling without really seeing it and dreading the day ahead. My heart was thumping and my limbs felt as if they were filled with cement but in the end I couldn't put it off any longer.

I checked on Gran, made tea and showered. I tilted my head back, closed my eyes and let the water run all over my face and hair. It was calming. By the time I got back into my bedroom and sat down at the dressing table to blank out a spot which kept re-emerging on my chin, I was feeling more in control.

"You *can* do this," I said to myself, staring straight into the mirror. "You've got to think about Mum. You haven't got a choice."

"Got to do what?" Dad poked his head around the half open door, taking my breath away.

"Where have you been?"

"At the hospital, watching over your mother." He held up his hands. "From a safe distance this time. She had no idea I was there."

"How is she this morning?"

"Still a bit woozy."

He came and stood behind me but I couldn't see his reflection in the mirror at all.

"What have you got to do that sounds so serious?" he asked.

I bit my lip. "Dad, I'm glad that you're here.

313

I want to say something."

I twisted on the stool to look at him. I wasn't going to do this staring into space. He didn't say anything. I opened my mouth, tried to find the words. They were there on the tip of my tongue but not in the right order. I had to say this properly, to get this sentence out in a sensitive and dignified way. But I couldn't. My voice just froze.

"Laura, I want to say something too." He knelt down in front of me. "I think that I ought to go back."

"To the hospital?"

He shook his head. "No, my darling princess. You know I didn't mean that."

I couldn't look at him. "But I don't want you to go."

"And believe me, I don't want to, but we both know that it's the right thing, don't we?"

I nodded. Tears fell onto my knees.

"Besides, you don't want me following you around for the rest of your life, commenting on your boyfriends or hassling you about your homework. You've got to live your life without me, Laura."

"I don't know how to do that. I've never known

how to do that."

And then, for the first time, he took my hands in his. His strange molecular fingers wrapped around mine. We waited for something to happen, a crack of thunder like they have in films or a deep angry voice from above. But there was nothing like that, just Dad's love for me spreading up my arms and through my body, and mine for him flowing back into his form.

"All you have to do, Laura, is be yourself. You are the kindest, most beautiful, caring girl on the planet and I am so proud of you."

"If I'd gone to the farmers' market with Mum this wouldn't have happened," I gulped.

"Yes it would, eventually. Deep down we've both always known I couldn't stay around for ever, haven't we?"

I nodded. It was true.

"Now that your gran knows I'm here and so does the vicar and Sam, the decision has been made for me."

"I didn't want to have to send you away."

"And you haven't. I've decided this myself.

Besides, I'll be up there looking down on you, trying to protect you, making sure you don't get into any trouble. Promise me you'll be careful, Laura. You won't take silly risks?"

"I'll try not to."

"You still don't understand how much I worry about you, do you? It's like having one of those balls made up of rubber bands inside your chest. Each band is a thread of fear and they're all wound around each other, tangled up. You think that the ball will get smaller as your child grows up but it's not like that. The more you watch them changing and going out into the world, the bigger it gets."

I managed a smile. "You're not the only one who worries, you know. Will you be all right going back there? I don't know anything about The Other Side. I don't know if you're happy there."

"Yes, sweetheart, I shall be happy, even more so because I've spent this time with you."

"It'll be nice to know that you're there watching over me," I murmured.

"Always. I'll be with you every second."

"Oh, right..."

He pulled his hand away and slapped his forehead. The molecules splished out to the side like a starburst.

"No," he said, returning my smile, "actually not quite that much. After all, a girl needs some privacy, doesn't she?"

I nodded.

"See," he said, a touch triumphantly. "I'm learning. You've taught me a lot, Laura."

"You've taught me a lot too," I whispered. "Thank you."

He stretched his hands up my arms. I moved closer. It felt good but it still wasn't a proper hug.

"Silly girl," he said softly, his lips almost touching my hair. "You don't have to thank me. That's what proper fathers do."

He bent his head closer, our foreheads millimetres apart.

"Now, remember, even when you can't see me, I'm still here for you. When I've gone you can talk to me, tell me your troubles and find a quiet space to listen for the answers. Love is eternal, Laura. I will never really leave you, you know that, don't you?"

"Yes." And then the question I had to ask. "When will you go?"

"Before your mum comes out of hospital, if possible. I wasn't lying when I said that I didn't know how to do the return journey. I'm going to need a bit of help. Can you sort that out for me?"

He was trying to make it easier for me, trying to lessen the pain. But then that's what good fathers do, isn't it?

SACRIFICE

"Gran, we've got a problem."

She looked up from her sewing. She was taking up the hem of one of my dresses. Mum had said it was more than short enough when I bought it but Gran agreed to taking it up by another five centimetres if it would persuade me to wear it instead of shoving it to the back of my wardrobe.

"I knew it!" she mumbled. "He's going to be difficult."

Her face took on that mean expression that she used to have, the one that I hadn't seen for a few weeks, but to be fair she had got a couple of pins in the corner of her mouth. I was worried to death she might swallow them.

"No, it's not like that, but he does need help."

I explained the situation but she still looked doubtful as to whether it was really true.

She put down the sewing, took the pins out and looked around the room.

"Where is he now?"

"Upstairs."

I listened, chewing little bits from my nails, as Gran rang Reverend Tim.

"When will you come?" Gran asked him.

Her eyes flickered over to me. I saw relief but also sorrow in the quiver of her lips.

"How long have we got?" I asked when she pressed the button to end the call. She wasn't on the phone for long but by the time she'd finished, all that hard work I'd put into growing my nails had been undone.

"Not long. Apparently they never work alone with this sort of thing so provided he can get someone else to help him out they'll be here this afternoon."

"That soon?" In my naivety I'd thought it would take at least a day to organise.

"You've got to be brave, Laura."

"I'll try."

"I know you will. You don't think he'll change his mind?"

I wondered for a moment how well I really knew Dad. How much of a difference these last few weeks had made to our relationship.

"No," I said with certainty. "I'm sure he won't."

"We'll just have to hope not," Gran replied. "It will make it much easier if he cooperates."

"He will. He's doing this for me. He won't let me down."

Before I got the chance to disappear upstairs to find Dad, there was a knock at the back door. It was Sam.

"My dad told me what's going to happen. I wanted to see if you were okay," he said.

"No, not really."

He reached out and touched my arm. I felt a little better. We went and sat on the swing seat.

"Will you be here?" I asked.

"If you want me to be."

I nodded. "Yes please."

"How's your mum?"

"She's okay but they want to keep her in for another day. Dad wants to have gone before she comes back from the hospital."

"Probably a good idea."

I looked up at the sky. "I bet your mum's up there somewhere, watching over you."

"Do you think so?"

"Yes, I'm sure of it."

"Do you think your dad would take a message to her?"

"I can ask him."

"I wish my mum would come back and see me," Sam said, "just to let me know that she's okay. Sometimes when I come back from school I expect to find her in the kitchen, making a pot of tea and taking biscuits out of the oven. I don't know why because she never lived in the house we're in now. But it still seems empty without her."

"It's funny," I said, "but even though I've lived without Dad for years and years and he's only been back in my life for a few weeks, I'll miss him so much when he's gone."

"My dad says that just because Mum's gone doesn't mean she isn't still a part of our lives. We talk about her all the time. I think about her every day. I still love her even though I can't hold her or see her.

I'll always love her just like you'll always love your dad."

"Doorbell, Laura." Dad stood up and pulled his shirt down at the sides, fiddled with the collar so it was straight. Downstairs I heard Gran fumbling with the catch on the front door.

"This is it then," I said.

"Not quite," he said. "There's one more thing I need to do. Come here."

So I stepped forwards until we were almost touching and he folded his arms around me. It felt like being wrapped in the softest, warmest blanket. It was all the hugs I had missed over the years rolled into one. It was generous and open and completely unconditional. It felt like love in its purest form. Everyone should have a hug like that at some time in their life. As I felt all of Dad's love envelop me I knew that this moment would be one I would remember for ever. This feeling of absolute safety would keep me going when life got hard. This was what I had been searching for ever since he died. We stood there in stillness, him resting his chin on the top of my head, me resting my face against his chest.

"Promise me something, Laura," Dad muttered into my hair.

I didn't reply, didn't want to break the magic. He moved away slightly, blew the hair from my face, so so gently.

"Promise me that you'll keep in touch with Daisy. Promise me that you'll be happy."

"I promise."

And he smiled the saddest of smiles and clasped me to him all over again. "My darling, darling Laura," he whispered. "You will never know how much I love you."

"But I do," I replied. "Because it's just as much as I love you."

There was the lightest of taps on my door.

"Laura, are you there?" Sam's voice was barely above a whisper. "They're waiting for you downstairs."

I opened the door.

"Is everything okay?" he asked, his gaze shooting over my shoulder.

"Everything's fine. We're both ready."

It was rubbish, of course. I wasn't ready at all. How could I be? I straightened up, tried to loosen my shoulders a little, fixed a half smile to my face, partly for Dad's benefit, partly for my own.

"Let's go," I said, sounding a lot more controlled than I felt.

"Wait!" Dad said.

"What is it?" Suddenly I wasn't so sure that he could go through with it. He glanced at Sam as if willing him away.

"Can you give us a minute?" I asked but Sam was already sliding out of the door.

Dad twirled a bit of my hair around his finger. "I just wanted to say, Laura, that he's okay, your Sam. I was wrong about him."

Your Sam. Those words made my heart do a little leap.

"I'm not sure that he's mine," I said.

Dad lifted my chin with his fingers.

"He's yours, sweetheart. I'm convinced of it. Don't you let him get away. You might regret it."

I smiled softly. "I'll do my best to hang on to him then."

"Good," Dad said. "And I know you'll look after your mother for me and…" he hesitated, "… if she does find someone else, I won't mind too much."

"We'll all be fine, Dad," I said. "You mustn't worry."

And he took hold of my hand for the last time.

Reverend Tim was in the sitting room talking to another man. They both wore casual trousers, short-sleeved shirts and dog collars. I'd expected them to be all dressed up in cassocks, as if they were conducting a church service, but I was glad they weren't. It made the whole process seem a bit more normal, which is ridiculous because what can be less normal than getting a spirit to leave your house, especially when it's someone you know and love?

"There you are, dear," Gran said, standing up and shuffling over to put her arm around my shoulders.

Reverend Tim introduced the other vicar. We shook hands. He gave me a sort of pitying look.

I half smiled at him, wondering why *I* felt the need to reassure everyone.

"Now then, dear," Gran said, giving me a little squeeze, "where exactly is *the problem* at the moment?"

"He's here, Gran," I replied. "Right beside us."

Dad puffed out his cheeks and blew softly at the side of Gran's head so that a tendril of hair came loose from one of her clips.

"Oh," she said, looking slightly alarmed, "so he is."

I looked up at everyone. Even the two vicars had shadows passing across their faces and they must have been used to this sort of thing.

"It's okay. He won't cause any trouble."

"Laura," Dad whispered in my ear, "just check that it won't hurt. I'm not any good with pain."

I asked the question and Reverend Tim assured us that, if Dad cooperated, there shouldn't be any difficulties. He placed a small black box upon the coffee table. Wedged under the handle was a beautiful wooden cross. Flowers and birds and butterflies were painted on it in bright, clear colours. Once opened, I could see that the box had a sapphire-blue lining and contained a miniature communion set. Reverend Tim spread the pieces out on a white linen cloth. There was a little glass decanter with a silver rim which contained communion wine, a small silver chalice, a round box for those bread wafers that Gran says always get stuck to the roof of your mouth, and a dish that Reverend Tim said was a paten. When everything was arranged, the other vicar asked if we were ready to begin, or if Dad and I needed a few more moments. Dad looked at me and his face was so sad that I could hardly bear to look back.

"No," I said. "We've said all there is to say."

We began by gathering around the front door, Dad close by my side.

"Peace be to this house and all who dwell in it," Reverend Tim said in a clear, authoritative voice. He blessed the front door and splashed it with some holy water which he had in a little blue pot. The splashing was done with what looked like an ordinary pastry brush from the supermarket. We moved through the house as Reverend Tim encouraged God's presence and said prayers from a slim red leather-bound book. There was a different prayer for each room of the house but in one way or another they all asked for God's blessing and peace. Dad was so close to me as we moved from room to room and Gran kept a slight distance, as if she knew that we needed our space, this last time together as father and daughter. We spent longer in my room while Reverend Tim splashed the chair where Dad had sat. I felt Dad shiver then, saw his molecules ripple like a churning stream. There was a pause as everyone seemed to sense his sudden distress.

"Are you okay?" I murmured and he nodded, smiled but the smile didn't reach his eyes.

Reverend Tim moved on to the wardrobe. He splashed my bed, the curtains, the dressing table, the carpet, all the time spreading his prayers into every available space. Finally, when everything had received a good soaking and Reverend Tim seemed satisfied, we went back downstairs to the sitting room and I knew that the time was getting near. Dad must have known too because he moved away from me and stood in a corner on the other side of the room. Alone. When I went to join him he shook his head and put up his hand to stop me. Already it felt as if he had left me. I could still see him but he looked unreachable, detached, desolate. I stood in the middle of the room with everyone watching me and I was acutely aware of everything and everyone. Yet I didn't feel part of it. I was separate. I was empty. I wanted it all to be over but at the same time I wanted to hang on to the moment. Impossible. Why did I always want the impossible?

I'm not sure who moved first but I became aware of Gran kneeling down at the coffee table, and the soft murmur of the other vicar's voice as he gave her communion.

"Laura." Reverend Tim touched me on the shoulder. He gestured to the table, to the wine and to the bread. "Do you want to?" he asked.

I looked up into his face. It was so kind, so full of concern.

"I'm not confirmed."

"It doesn't matter."

No, I thought, not much does matter really, does it? All of those silly rules and pressures we put ourselves under. At the end of the day there are very few things that really matter, that are really important. So I moved to the table, as if in a trance. I thought it might help, doing something, reminding my body that although Dad was disappearing I was still here.

Gran's right. The wafers do get stuck to the roof of your mouth. As I knelt in front of the coffee table, trying to curl my tongue around that wafer and free it, I kept one eye on Dad. He was becoming more translucent. I could barely see the edge of him against the flowery pattern of the curtains. Reverend Tim held the chalice to my lips and I took a sip of the earthy-tasting wine. I only averted my eyes for a second but when I looked up Dad was barely there. Despite all of my efforts the wafer was still stuck to the roof of my mouth and the wine felt rough against my throat. I could smell Gran's perfume, a drift of lavender, and outside a bird, maybe a magpie, made a harsh cawing sound.

No, I wanted to shout. Stop! Don't do this. But I couldn't speak. I stayed kneeling while Reverend Tim read a passage from the Bible. I was afraid that if I moved Dad would have gone and it would all be over. But I wanted it to be over, didn't I? As if he knew what I was thinking, Sam knelt down beside me and linked his arm through mine and I let those beautiful, lyrical, comforting words wrap themselves around me like a hug.

"In the beginning was the Word, and the Word was with God, and the Word was God. He was with God in the beginning. Through him all things were made; without him nothing was made that has been made. In him was life and that life was the light of men. The light shines in the darkness..."

My eyes were full of tears now. I kept blinking them away, trying to keep Dad in my sight but he was leaving me. He didn't have any feet now and I could see his legs disappearing like early morning mist when it meets sunlight. Sam squeezed my arm tighter and on the other side I reached behind me and gripped Gran's hand, hard. Reverend Tim called out Dad's name in full.

"Gareth James Cooper," he said, adding more prayers asking for forgiveness, repentance and resting in peace. When he finished speaking the room was like a calm pool. Even the frantic beating of my heart had slowed, the churning in my brain settled down and strangely the emptiness had gone.

Suddenly everything seemed as if it would be all right. In the corner Dad lifted his hand and waved. I let go of Sam's clasp and waved back.

"I love you, Laura."

The words swished around the room like one of those ribbons gymnasts use, up and down, in and out. They were all the colours of the rainbow, their edges sparkling like glitter. Everyone heard them. I could tell. Maybe not with their ears but in their hearts.

"I love you too, Dad," I mouthed. "Don't forget to take that message to Sam's mum."

Just in time. The second I finished, my daddy had gone.

UNDERSTANDING

That night I lay in bed looking at the chair where Dad had sat. I half expected him to appear with a 'ta-da, you can't get rid of me that easily' expression on his face but really I knew that he wouldn't. As I listened to Gran's longcase clock chime a quarter to three, I was sure that, only a few days short of the anniversary of his death, Dad had well and truly gone. The house felt different. Gran felt it too. Although she couldn't see him, the second he disappeared she let out a long sigh. We had all stayed very still for a few moments, like those living statues you get in tourist towns, waiting, listening, watching. I'd expected to feel heavy with sadness but I didn't. Of course I was upset but at the same time I felt lighter. By coming back, by blowing away the story I had built up over the years, Dad had given me a precious gift. For the first time in my life I knew who I was. I felt free to be me.

After Dad had gone we'd had tea. The scones Gran had made earlier in the day were untouched. No one spoke much. Then Reverend Tim drove Gran and me to see Mum. Sam didn't come. He said he'd got something to do at home. I was a bit disappointed not to have him sitting there beside me.

Mum was sitting up in bed reading a magazine when we got there. The concussion seemed to have gone but the doctor wanted her to stay in hospital for one more night.

"You look a bit peaky, Laura," she fretted.

"I'm fine, Mum. Don't worry."

Gran leaned forward from the chair and patted my knee. "We make a good team, Laura and I," she said.

"Really?" Mum sounded surprised. She lay back against the pillow. "Maybe I'll just stay here for a few more days then and get some rest," she said with a grin. "Actually, on second thoughts, I don't think I will. The food's awful. I've not been sleeping properly either. I've had the strangest dreams. I dreamed that Gareth was here, sitting in that chair right next to my bed." She shook her head as if trying to get rid of the image. "And when I woke up it all seemed so real, almost as if it hadn't been a dream at all."

Gran pursed her lips together. "Bumps on the head can do funny things to you," she said.

"Obviously," Mum replied. "In all the years since... since he left us, I've barely dreamed of him at all and never like that, never so clearly."

She shook out her fringe and winced, lifting her hand to her head.

"It's the most ridiculous thing but I almost wondered if he'd come back, you know, as a ghost." She laughed. "Listen to me. That bang on the head has sent me around the bend. Talking of around the bend, what's happened to the car?"

"Written off I'm afraid," Gran said.

"I have no idea what happened," Mum said. "I remember swerving to avoid a pheasant and just losing control."

"Maybe there was something wrong with the steering," I said to Mum.

"Good thing the car can't be salvaged in that case," Gran said.

Mum turned to Gran and suddenly she looked like a little girl again. "I can't bear to think what might have happened."

"Then don't," Gran said briskly. "Think about coming home instead. Tim's offered to come and fetch you if you're happy with that."

"Oh," Mum said and I thought I spotted the slightest blush rising up from her jawline, "that's kind of him. He's been so good and he's such a busy man, I really don't want to take any more of his time."

"I don't think he minds at all," Gran said, a touch conspiratorially.

"Mother," Mum said, "what *are* you up to? I do hope you haven't press-ganged him into this?"

"Of course not. He offered, didn't he, Laura?"

I nodded.

Mum looked from one to the other of us.

"Well I don't want you getting any ideas, either of you. The poor man only lost his wife a year or so ago. We're just friends."

"Did I suggest anything else?" Gran asked, looking quite put out. Then she turned to me and winked.

* * *

Reverend Tim was due to pick Mum up from hospital sometime during the morning, after the doctors had done their rounds and discharged her. I decided not to go with him. Instead Gran and I made a fish pie for lunch as it's one of Mum's favourites. Gran sat at the table peeling mushrooms while I popped the mixed fish in the oven for a few minutes and began to make the white sauce. The butter was sizzling in the saucepan and Gran had the radio turned up quite loudly so neither of us heard the knock at the back door.

I was miles away, thinking of Dad and wondering what he was doing, if he was looking down on us. There was a sharp tap on the window above the sink, which made me jump and scatter the wooden spoonful of cornflour all down my navy T-shirt. Sam pressed his face to the glass and grinned. He looked really silly, all mouth and nose. I grinned and pulled the butter off the heat slightly before going to let him in. He had a large box under one arm. It said 'Interflora' on the side.

"Ah, Samuel," Gran said, "what a nice surprise and some flowers too."

He put the box down in a corner of the kitchen and I returned to my sauce.

"Isn't it a nice surprise to see Sam, Laura?"

"Yes," I replied, making a second attempt to stir in the cornflour, and wondering why she was suddenly behaving rather oddly. "Of course."

"Why don't you come and sit down for a moment, dear?"

I presumed that she was talking to Sam but when I turned around to see if he wanted something to drink, he was already sitting down and they were both staring at me expectantly.

"Me?" I asked.

"Yes, dear, you," Gran said. "Let's have a little break."

"I can't leave this sauce now," I said, tipping in the milk, "or it will go all lumpy."

"There are more important things than lumpy sauce, Laura," Gran said, grinning from ear to ear, "but if you must carry on, we can wait."

Wait? Wait for what? For me to sit down? What was this weirdness?

As soon as the sauce thickened to just the right

consistency I took the pan off the heat and put it to one side, placing a piece of damp greaseproof paper across the top to stop a skin forming.

"Do you want a drink?" I asked Sam.

"In a minute."

As I sat down Sam stood up and moved towards the box. Flowers! Had he really bought *me* flowers? No one had ever done that before.

"I thought they were for Mum," I said.

"Close your eyes, Laura," he said, "and hold out your hands."

My heart began to beat faster as a memory came flooding back. He had used exactly the same words once before. I listened to the scrape of cardboard as he opened the box, waited for the rustle of cellophane. Don't let there be any, I thought. Stop it, Laura. You know it's flowers. It says so on the box. The only sound was the slight squeak of Sam's trainers as he crossed the quarry-tiled floor. He was standing in front of me now. I wanted to open my eyes but instead I screwed them up tight.

"Ready?" he asked.

I nodded.

And then I felt it – the softest fur. A small damp

nose, nudging my hand, and finally, as he placed her in my palms, I opened my eyes. Gloria looked up at me. I couldn't speak. There was this fullness in my chest. I just looked at Sam who was kneeling in front of me, one hand still on Gloria's back.

"I always knew that you didn't really want to part with her."

"No, I didn't," I whispered. "I thought she'd have found another home. I didn't dare ask, didn't want to find out."

"She's been with me at the vicarage." He looked over at Gran. "We've been waiting for the right time and we reckoned you might be feeling a bit low at the moment."

"Thank you," I said, tears streaming down my cheeks. "She's the best present I've ever had."

"And she's yours, Laura," Sam said, "for keeps this time."

I lifted Gloria to my face. "I promise," I whispered. "I will never ever let you down again."

Later, after lunch, when Gran and Mum and Tim were still sitting around the table talking, Sam and I took Gloria outside into the small, walled area to the side of the orchard. We sat on the grass while she chased a piece of string until she was worn out and then she flopped in a little furry heap on my lap. I couldn't stop looking at her, couldn't believe she was really here, was really mine.

"I'll never be able to thank you enough," I said to Sam.

"I know," he said with a grin. "You'll owe me for years and years."

I grinned back.

"You'll never be able to get rid of me because every day Gloria will give a little *miaow* as if to say, 'Have you remembered to thank Sam today?'"

"It's terrible, isn't it?" I said jokily. "We're stuck with each other. You're responsible for Gloria too. You're like her godfather. You'll have to keep an eye on her and check that I'm looking after her properly."

"I can think of worse people to be stuck with," Sam said.

I looked up at him, leaned a little closer.

Suddenly he looked unsure of himself. There was a guarded look in his eyes and I turned away slightly. Embarrassed for both of us. Maybe I'd misread the signs. Maybe he didn't like me as much as I liked him. Stupid Laura, I thought. Then, suddenly, his face was in front of mine, his freckled skin and sandy eyelashes millimetres away. With Gloria fast asleep on my knee and Mum's laughter drifting over the wall from the kitchen, he leaned forwards and kissed me on the lips. I could tell from that kiss that Dad was right. It *was* me Sam liked, after all.

The next day I went to visit Liberty. I hadn't seen her to talk to since she turned up in my bedroom and suggested we collected the eggs together. I'd seen her in the car with her mum and I'd seen her that day when she was with Sam. It's not that I hadn't tried to meet up with her. I'd texted several times but she was always busy and then I had more important things on my mind with Dad. It seemed strange to be walking through the village without him by my side and for a second I wanted him there telling me that I was doing the right thing, that Liberty wouldn't bite my head off or, even worse, just ignore me.

"If you're up there, Dad," I murmured towards

343

the clear blue sky, "I could do with a bit of help here."

Outside Liberty's front door I stood for a moment, trying to compose myself, trying to remember what I'd been planning to say. I was just about to knock when the door swung open.

"Laura!" Aunt Jane slapped her hand to her chest. "You made me jump."

"Sorry."

We stood there for a second, sizing each other up.

"How's your mother?" she asked.

"Okay, a bit bruised and achey but she's glad to be home."

Aunt Jane's eyes filled with tears. "It could have been so much worse."

"Yes."

"I'll pop around later. I did go to the hospital, you know."

"I know."

She stared at me for a moment before stepping forwards and wrapping me in a hug. I tensed, kept my arms by my sides.

"Can you forgive me, Laura? I've behaved very badly. Sometimes it takes something like this to shake you up, to help you sort out your priorities."

She was holding me so tightly I could barely breathe, let alone speak.

"Everything's going to be all right from now on."

I nodded. She held me away slightly.

"It's so wonderful having you and Liz here. She's doing such a good job with Mother."

"I think she'd like you to tell her that."

She stroked my cheek. "I have, I have. And I'll keep on saying it to try to make up for being so stressed and difficult. We're not a big family, Laura. We need each other, don't we?"

"Yes," I whispered. "We do."

Another rib-crushing came, as if by making her hug so strong she could let me know how sorry she felt. I just hoped she really meant it. I thought she did.

"So," she said, standing back again and giving me some breathing space, "have you come to see Liberty? You two haven't spent much time together since you got here."

"No," I replied. "I mean, yes, I have come to see her. If she wants to."

Aunt Jane frowned. "Why on earth wouldn't she want to? You two are like sisters." She laughed, her face suddenly flustered. "And sisters fall out sometimes. You know that. But it's never for long. In fact, she was going to come and see you later."

Aunt Jane grabbed my hand.

"Don't blame her too much for not telling you, Laura. She was only doing as we asked."

I nodded and she stroked my head.

"You two have always been such good friends. Don't let this come between you."

I followed her into the hall and we both stopped at the bottom of the stairs.

"Do you want to go up?" she suggested.

I looked towards the landing and bit my lip.

"I tell you what, I'll call her, shall I?" Aunt Jane offered. "Liberty!" she yelled at the top of her voice. "You've got a visitor."

There was no sound of movement from upstairs. Aunt Jane smiled at me and squeezed my arm.

"I know she's up there. She's probably got her earphones in."

Or maybe she just doesn't want to see me,

I thought. Maybe she thinks I'll be mad with her. And she's right. What *am* I doing here? She should be the one coming to me.

"Liberty!" Aunt Jane yelled again.

This time I saw a chink of light as Liberty's door was pulled open and then, as I looked up, she leaned over the banisters.

"Look who's here," Aunt Jane said in a falsely jolly voice. "Isn't this a nice surprise?"

"Hi," I said.

I couldn't read Liberty's face at all. Was she surprised to see me, pleased, wary or a combination of all three? Suddenly I wished that I hadn't come.

"Why don't you go up," Aunt Jane said. It wasn't really a question because she shoved me lightly in the small of my back. "I'll bring you some tea and I've just baked some biscuits."

Before I had the chance to say no, she had gone, flurrying back to the kitchen. Liberty and I looked at each other. We both started to speak at the same time. It broke the ice a bit.

"I'm sorry," she said, dropping the words onto

the top of my head. "I'm sorry I didn't tell you what I knew. I should have."

And in that moment I forgave her. Standing in that narrow, dark hall, my hand clutching the oak banister for support, I saw what a difficult position she'd been in. It was as easy as that.

"I haven't known for long and I hated keeping it from you," she said, as I sat on her bed and bit into a warm cookie. "I overheard Mum and Dad talking one night when I went downstairs to get a glass of water. They made me promise not to say anything."

She looked so upset. She sat forwards on a small stool, her hands clenched together, her forehead all pinched.

"We've always said that we're like sisters," she whispered, "so I should have ignored them. I should have told you anyway. I don't blame you if you hate me."

"Of course I don't hate you," I said. "I'm sorry you had to hide it from me but, to be honest, if I'd been in your shoes I don't know what I'd have done. Probably the same as you."

"Really?" She lifted her head, looked at me

properly for the first time.

I nodded.

"Your dad must have been horrible to behave like that."

"No," I said, "you're wrong."

She looked surprised. And I so wanted to tell her but I couldn't, not yet. It was my turn to have a secret and I wasn't doing it as a form of revenge but just because I wasn't ready to go through it all again. I knew that describing everything in words would bring it all back and I felt too fragile for that.

"He wasn't a bad man, Liberty," I said. "He just got himself into a bit of a mess. He made a mistake and we can all do that."

"But you've got a sister?"

"Yes. She's called Daisy. I've met her and she's lovely."

Her face crumpled a little.

"Not lovelier than you though," I said with a slightly jokey tone. "You'll always be my 'sister' too."

She half smiled at that. "I'm sorry what I said, about you always getting extra money and presents from Gran. It wasn't fair."

I paused.

"I know you're her favourite, Liberty, and that's okay. I can live with that."

Her mouth fell open. "Me? Her favourite? You're kidding, aren't you? When you were back in London all she did was talk about you. To be honest I've always felt a little bit jealous.

"But when I came up here, she was always so mean to me, or that's how it seemed."

"Maybe she just didn't want to show that *you* were 'the special one'."

We looked at each other and laughed. And as we laughed I felt something inside of me relax. Liberty sat up straighter.

"I'm sorry, Laura. I know that I've been horrible. I didn't want it to be like this. Mum was so stressed and I felt as if I had to take sides. It wasn't how I imagined it would be. I thought we'd all have a great time together once you moved up here."

"Me too," I whispered.

Her eyes had pooled with tears. "Can we start again?"

I nodded. "That would be good."

She stood up and we hugged. I wasn't stupid. It wasn't all going to be sweetness and light from now on, especially when I told her about Sam. But things had changed between us. *We* had changed. I felt that whatever life threw at us we'd be able to work our way through any problems and that we'd always be there for each other. Of that I was sure.

THE BEGINNING

I went back to London at October half-term. I was spending one night with Penny and one night with Abi. Penny met me at St Pancras station. I'd told her not to bother but she insisted. We hugged and she took hold of my case.

"I'm so glad you've come," she said, turning to look at me as we went down the escalator. "Daisy's really looking forward to getting to know you better. She talked of nothing else when I saw her last weekend."

To be honest, at that moment, I just wanted to turn around, push my way past all of the people and run back up towards the platform. This could be a complete disaster, I thought. It's one thing having a few random conversations with someone by text or telephone but quite another meeting face to face. When we spoke it was all a bit stilted and I began to doubt if we'd ever form a proper bond. What if we had nothing in common? What if we found that we didn't really like each other? What if every time I looked at Daisy she just reminded me of the fact that Dad had betrayed Mum? What if I couldn't be the big sister she wanted me to be? Mum and Aunt Jane may argue a lot but there's this invisible thread that always pulls them back together, always encourages them to make up. Daisy and I didn't seem to have that thread. I wondered if we would meet up once a year just because we had a father in common and not because we really wanted to spend time with each other. It was like this pressure weighing down on me all of the time. Sometimes I thought it would have been better if I'd never found out about her at all.

Penny waited until we were walking past the shops, towards the Underground, before draping her arm lightly around my shoulders.

"It's okay to feel nervous," she said, "but it'll be fine. Trust me. Just take it one step at a time.

It was almost exactly what Gran had said to me as she kissed me on the cheek that morning and pressed a tiny sprig of white heather into my palm.

 353

"For good luck," she whispered, "not that I think you'll need it."

I never thought that I'd say this, but I'll miss Gran when we move out of the farm. She's getting stronger by the day and Mum says that after Christmas we could probably start looking for a little cottage for just the two of us. It won't be too far away so hopefully I can still nip in and see Gran after school. She always has tea and cake ready for me and she keeps an eye on Gloria when I'm not around. I can tell her some of my worries and she doesn't get all het up like Mum does. Gran just sits and listens quietly and then puts everything into perspective.

"Thanks, Gran," I'd said, tucking the heather into my jeans pocket. "But I think you're wrong there. I think I'm going to need all of the luck I can get."

"Laura, sweetheart," she'd replied, stroking my cheek, "this is just the beginning. Things take time to settle down and you've had a lot of big changes to deal with. Don't expect too much too soon."

I tried to keep those words of Gran's in my head as I unpacked a few of my things at Penny's and picked at the lunch she'd made. She chatted on cheerfully about her work and asked me about the farm and Gloria and Mum. I just kept looking at the clock.

"I wish your mum could have come too. Not to be here this afternoon," Penny said, turning and handing me a plate to dry up. "Obviously that would have been too difficult, but I would like us to meet up again."

"She's working," I replied. "She's got some freelance jobs which she's really enjoying."

"That's good," Penny said. "Maybe next time."

I nodded. "Maybe."

Penny threw me a wistful smile. "Your dad would have been so proud of you, Laura, doing this. You do know that, don't you?"

"Yes," I said. "I know."

The doorbell went on the dot of half past two. Penny had just gone upstairs to make some notes for a new project she was working on. I knew she'd done that on purpose. Adults can be so obvious sometimes.

"Can you answer the door, please, Laura?" she called. "I'll be down in a minute."

I took a deep breath but my hands were shaking

as I fiddled with the brass catch. Daisy was standing very close to Amanda, their coat sleeves crumpled together, and they both looked as nervous as I felt.

"Hello, Laura," Amanda said. "How are you?"

"Fine, thanks."

Such a lie. I was far from fine. I concentrated on what Gran had said, "Don't expect too much too soon."

"Hi, Daisy," I said with a weak smile. "Are you okay?"

She nodded, looked up at me shyly as they walked past into the hall. I was so relieved when Penny padded down the stairs and hugged them both. Her natural warmth seemed to thaw the awkwardness a little.

"Laura's bought you a present," she said to Daisy. "Isn't that lovely? Do you want to go upstairs and see it? Then we'll have tea in a little while. Laura's grandma has sent some lovely lemon biscuits that she made."

Daisy hesitated so, tentatively, I held out my hand. She took hold of it and followed me up the stairs.

It was Mum's idea to buy something, which

I thought was pretty generous of her.

"It'll break the ice," she had said.

And she was right. As Daisy unwrapped the little parcel of glittery nail polish, her eyes lit up.

"I can do them for you, if you like," I offered.

So we sat on the bed together while I painted her nails and gradually she opened up.

"Do you miss London?" she asked.

"Yes," I replied, "but I'm getting used to Derbyshire. I've got my cousin Liberty down the road and I've just started at a new school."

"I'm starting at a new school next year," she said. "Is it scary?"

"A bit. But you'll be fine."

"Have you made new friends?"

"A few, but making good friends takes time. You can't rush it."

She wafted her fingers around to get the nails to dry.

"They look so pretty," she said. "Thank you, Laura."

"You're welcome," I said. "You can do mine if you like."

"Can I?"

Her eyes shone.

"Really? Tell me what colour you'd like."

"You choose," I said.

She picked each of the six bottles up and looked at them carefully. Then she looked at what I was wearing.

"I think you should wear purple," she said, "because it matches the birds on your top."

"Perfect," I said.

"Have you got any pets?" she asked, as I rested my hand on her knee.

I told her about Gloria and how she loved to chase things – butterflies, bees, bits of string, leaves.

Daisy laughed and the nail polish wavered onto my finger.

"Oops!" she said. "Sorry!"

"That's all right," I chuckled. "I do that all the time."

"Did your Mum get you Gloria?" she asked.

"No, a friend. He's called Sam."

She looked up at me and bit her lip.

"Is he your boyfriend?"

I nodded.

"That's a very special present. He must like you a lot."

I felt myself blushing. "He's a special person. He knew I'd always wanted a cat, ever since I was little."

"When our daddy was alive?"

"Yes. He was allergic to cats."

"I know. Mummy told me that. Do you remember him?"

"Yes."

"What was he like?"

I leaned back against the headboard and closed my eyes for a second. "He was funny and kind and silly sometimes."

"He sounds nice."

"He was."

"Did you love him a lot?"

"Yes."

She must have seen the tears welling up in my eyes.

"Does thinking about him make you sad?"

"Sometimes."

"I don't want you to be sad."

I leaned forwards and wiped my eyes. "No, me neither."

She put her arms around me. Her hair smelled of strawberry shampoo and her fingers tapped softly against my shoulder blades.

"Do you mind me putting flowers on his grave?" she whispered.

"No!"

I moved away slightly, looked into her anxious blue eyes. And at that moment something strange happened. I had this overwhelming desire to protect her from all harm. I didn't ever want to let her down.

"No, of course I don't. You have just as much right to put them there as I do."

"Why are your flowers always yellow?" she asked.

"Because it was Dad's favourite colour."

She was quiet for a moment. "I didn't know that. There's lots I don't know about him."

I stroked her hair away from her face. "Well maybe I can fill in some of the gaps."

She nodded, and carried on painting my nails without speaking.

"Would you like me to put some flowers on the grave from you sometimes?" she asked, putting the bottle of nail polish down on the bedside table.

"Do you know what I'd really like?" I replied.

She shook her head.

"I'd like you to put flowers on from both of us, one posy from Daisy and Laura. I think Dad would like that, don't you?"

She smiled. "I think if he's looking down on us," she said, "that would make him very happy."

I put my arms around her and clasped her close.

"I think so too."

I closed my eyes and pressed my lips to my sister's ear.

"I promise that I will always be here for you, Daisy."

It wasn't just a promise to my sister, it was a promise to our dad too.

Acknowledgements

A big thank-you to my editors Katie, Helen and Anne for their meticulous appraisals, support and encouragement. Also thanks to everyone at Templar who has been involved with the production of *No Going Back*. These are the unsung heroes of a published book but their hard work on my behalf is much appreciated.

Also thank you to Reverend Stephen Heygate from the Leicester Diocesan Deliverance Team who gave me valuable advice for certain scenes and also to Joseph Harris for putting me straight on molecular structure!

When Jess is knocked off her bike in a traffic accident, she finds herself at the gates of heaven before her destined death date.

Given one last chance to say goodbye, she heads back to earth in invisible form, to visit friends and family. But many secrets are revealed, and one shocking discovery presents Jess with the biggest choice she'll ever have to make.

'Such a poignant story for young teens that you can't help reading parts of it with a lump in your throat. Make sure you have your tissues at the ready'
'Book of the week', Manchester Evening News

'A heartwarming story that really makes you think about how well you know the ones you love'
Chicklish

I'm Suzy Puttock (yes, Puttock with a P), fourteen
years old and a total disaster magnet.
My life's full of ups and downs. My loved-up
big sister Amber's getting married and wants
lime-green bridesmaids' dresses. I'm not happy
about that. But there's this hot new guy, Zach, just
started at my school. I *am* happy about that.
Only . . . I've had a boyfriend
since forever - Danny.
So now I'm all kinds of confused!

'A hugely entertaining read'
Cathy Hopkins, author of *Million Dollar Mates*

'Will have you smiling like a lunatic'
Booktastic Reviews

Following a case of meningitis, teenager Demi is
pronounced profoundly deaf.
Suddenly, everything is different.
New school.
New friends.
Even a whole new language.
Can Demi learn to love the person
she has to become?

*'A coming-of-age tale with a twist . . . beautifully
written and thought-provoking'*
The Bookseller